Waiting for Her Isaac

By
Mr. and Mrs. Stephen B. Castleberry

Castleberry Farms Press

Cover art © was created by: Jeffrey T. Larson
11947 E. State Rd. 13 ● Maple, Wisconsin 54854
(715) 364-8473

All scripture references are from the King James Version of the Bible.

Second Edition
© Copyright 1997

Castleberry Farms Press
P.O. Box 337
Poplar, WI 54864

Printed in the U.S.A.

ISBN 1-891907-03-4

e-mail: cbfarmpr@pressenter.com

Visit us at: www.pressenter.com/~cbfarmpr

A Note From the Authors

Waiting for Her Isaac is the story of one young woman's spiritual preparation for marriage, as well as the story of her courtship. We hope this book will encourage young women to give themselves completely to the Lord as they wait for Him to unfold His plan for their lives.

As you read this novel, you'll learn a little about a ministry that our family has supported for years: The City of Youth in Campinas, Brazil. If you would like to learn more about this wonderful outreach you can write to Hope Unlimited International, 44 Montgomery Street, Suite 3730, San Francisco, California 94104. Email: hopeultd@aol.com. Web Site: www.hopeunlimited.org.

Our primary goal in publishing is to provide wholesome books in a manner that brings honor to our Lord. We are a homeschooling Christian family, and this is our family business. We always welcome your comments, suggestions, and most importantly, your prayers.

In the back of this book is information about the other titles we have published. If you would like to contact us, you can reach us at this address:

Mr. and Mrs. Stephen B. Castleberry
Castleberry Farms Press
P.O. Box 337
Poplar, WI 54864

Chapter One

*B*eth! Beth! Wake up, Beth! You've overslept again!" Beth Grant drowsily opened her eyes as her mother continued to shake her shoulder.

Eyes still heavy with sleep, she mumbled, "I'm sorry, Mom. What time is it?"

"It's only 6:30, but today is Ski Day, remember? You wanted us to get there early, so you wouldn't have to stand so long in line for the lift ticket."

Suddenly Beth sat up. "Ski Day! Oh, how could I have forgotten? I'll be right down!"

"Well, that's more like it!" laughed her mother. "Breakfast will be ready in about ten minutes." Mom left the room as Beth hurriedly began dressing.

Beth's bedroom was light and spacious. Her favorite colors of blue and white were obvious in the patchwork comforter on her white four-poster bed, the soft blue carpet on her floor, and the white priscilla curtains at the window. The early February day also seemed dressed in blue and white. Outside the window, the pale blue sky reflected soft blue shadows in the hollows of snow. Beth's eyes shone as she thought of the fun that lay ahead today.

But why did she have to be such a heavy sleeper? As she hastened out the door of her room, she glanced into the bedrooms of her brothers. As usual, they were all up ahead of her, beds made. Her bed! Uh-oh. Better go back and make it up quickly before Mom asked if she had remembered. Beth hoped for no more delays.

Running down the steps to the kitchen, she nearly collided with her father. "Oops! I'm sorry, Dad," Beth apologized. "I guess I was in too much of a hurry."

"Slow down a little, gal," replied her dad. "We won't leave for a while yet. I plan on having seconds on your mother's waffles. Have to have strength to face those slopes today." Dad grinned at Beth. "It's hard enough for an old man like me to keep up with you young people. Can't let myself faint with hunger halfway down the hill!"

Beth smiled back and gave Dad a hug. "You're not old! And thanks for taking us today, Dad. Ski Day is always one of the best days of the year."

"You're welcome, honey. But Beth, fifty-five is no spring chicken you know. I suppose you children will be expecting me to ski with you when I have to use canes for poles," Dad finished as they sat down.

After the blessing, everyone was too busy eating to do much talking, so Beth had time to observe her father closely and reflect a bit as she tried to finish her waffle. Dad probably was older than most of her friends' fathers, but he didn't seem old to Beth. He was such a happy, easygoing man. Small lines were etched at the outer corners of his eyes, crinkling frequently throughout the day. Beth had known instinctively what the phrase "laugh lines" meant the very first time she had read it. Dad's hair was gray, but he still had a young outlook on life. He enjoyed his children and their friends immensely, and tried to make sure his schedule was free to participate in all the family activities of their homeschool group. One Saturday every other month was chosen for these special activities. Beth enjoyed them all, but Ski Day was her favorite. The lodge chosen this year was a forty minute drive away, so she hoped Mom wouldn't insist that she finish her breakfast. Beth was much too excited to eat, and wished her family was already on the way.

Mom noticed her agitation and smiled at her daughter, who was staring forlornly at her half-filled plate. "Beth, try to

6

calm down a little. It's only a few minutes after seven, and the lift line doesn't even open until nine o'clock," Mom reminded her. "We still have the breakfast dishes to wash and lunches to pack before we leave. If you can't finish your breakfast, why don't you begin making the sandwiches?"

"Thanks, Mom," Beth smiled gratefully. "I really can't eat another bite."

"Well I sure can!" exclaimed ten-year-old Adam. "Are there anymore waffles, Mom?"

Beth held back a sigh. If Adam wanted another waffle, John was sure to want one too, and that would slow everything down. John was eight, and small for his age. He tried his best to eat everything Adam did, hoping to catch up to his brother.

"Adam, I'm sorry, but you've had two and I'm out of batter. We need to finish up anyway, because I think your father wanted to have family devotions before we leave. Is that right?" questioned Mom, turning to Dad.

Dad nodded. "Last year everyone was so exhausted from skiing that they could hardly stay awake for devotions after we got home. Let's read the Word now, if everyone has finished," suggested Dad. "Beth, come and sit down."

Dad opened his Bible and read, then each family member prayed aloud. Dad prayed last, asking the Lord to help each member of their family to represent Christ in their actions that day. Beth felt ashamed of herself for her impatient attitude and silently asked God's forgiveness. She felt much more at peace as she rose to help finish the kitchen work, and resolved to just enjoy the day as God brought it about.

Soon Dad and Michael, Beth's eighteen-year-old brother, had the van loaded and waiting at the front door. Everyone grabbed last-minute items and headed out the door, just as the clock struck eight. Beth relaxed. They would be there in plenty of time, and she had even remembered the playdough for Katie's little sisters. "What's that blue stuff?" asked John as he looked at the plastic bag on the seat beside Beth.

"Just some playdough I made for the Myers' little girls," answered Beth. "Katie and Mrs. Myers have been so busy all week that I told them I'd make some."

"I'm sure they wouldn't have had time to make any themselves. That was thoughtful of you, Beth," Mom commented.

"Their little girls are so cute," said Beth. "I wish I had a little sister. It seems as though all my friends have someone small in their family. It would be so much fun," finished Beth wistfully.

"I know, honey," Mom sympathized. "I often wish we had little ones too. But that wasn't God's plan for our family, and He knows best. You know that the Lord didn't have your father and I meet until we were a bit older, and we are just grateful for the four children that He blessed us with. Let's be thankful that He has given all of us to each other." Betty Grant was quiet a moment, then softly repeated, "Very thankful." Beth saw Mom's eyes take on a faraway look, and she wondered if her mother was thinking back eight years, to when they had almost lost John as a baby.

At two months of age, John's kidneys had failed, while they had been living as missionaries in Brazil. Over rough and bumpy roads, the family had ridden in an unreliable Jeep for six hours to get to the hospital in Belem. Beth had only been eight years old at the time, but she still remembered the fear she had felt for her baby brother as he lay so still and feverish in his mother's arms. The doctors in Belem had found the problem very quickly, and soon baby John was much better. Beth believed that was the result of prayers from many believers in the little village they had left behind. Weeks followed in which John had undergone many tests and treatments. Then the mission board had brought the Grant family back to the States, and Robert Grant had taken a job as assistant pastor in their present church. His heart was still the heart of a missionary, and Beth knew he was deeply saddened by the fact that he had never been able to return to Brazil. But Dad had accepted the move as God's will, and he always expressed his gratitude to the Lord for allowing John to live. At five years of age, John had received one of Dad's kidneys in a successful operation. Although John would always be a bit small for his age, he wasn't really much smaller than his friends. The medication he had to take regularly to prevent his body from rejecting the kidney, plus the need to be near good emergency care, would always require the Grants to live in the States. Dad kept in touch with many of his missionary friends, however, and the Grants often had them as visitors on furlough.

Michael had also missed missionary life when they returned to the States, but Beth had only dim memories of those years. She didn't remember much about Brazil, and couldn't imagine a happier life than what she had now. She loved living in their town, and all the like-minded friends she had there. Of course, not all the girls her age at church were like her, but a good many were. There was a large homeschooling group in town, mostly made up of families from their church and another large church. There were activities she could attend twice a month or so with her brothers and Mom, plus the six family days a year that the fathers tried to attend.

Beth's best friend was Katie Myers, who attended the same church as the Grants. Katie was sixteen, just Beth's age, and was the oldest of eight children. Katie certainly didn't have a bedroom of her own, but she didn't mind being a bit crowded. She was a cheerful, gentle sister who obviously enjoyed helping her mom care for the younger children in the family. Her three youngest sisters were only two, four, and six years old, and they were the little girls for whom Beth had made the playdough. Even though Beth didn't have small brothers or sisters of her own, Mom encouraged her to be a blessing to the other families they knew with little ones, by helping them any way she could.

Beth and Katie shared many of the same beliefs and hopes for the future. Both looked forward to the day when they would be wives and mothers themselves, "keepers at home," as they often reminded each other. They also encouraged each other in their wish for courtship, and several of the other girls in their homeschool group had the same convictions. Beth looked forward to spending today with these friends.

As they pulled into the parking lot of the ski lodge, Beth silently thanked God for His many blessings. How grateful she was for the life God had chosen to give her!

Chapter Two

The next few months passed quickly for Beth. Spring arrived early that year in eastern Tennessee, and the April homeschool picnic occurred on a warm, sunny Saturday. Beth and Katie, along with Jessica Lawson, Rachel Keck, and Emily Weeks, followed a small stream far down a gentle slope. There the stream leveled off and widened into a shallow bed of gravel, water sparkling in the sunlight. Pulling off socks and shoes, the girls waded into the icy stream, gasping and laughing as the cold water ran over their feet.

It was Emily who saw the flowers first. On the far bank was a grassy meadow filled with violets and mayflowers. They seemed to beckon to the girls. Exclamations of delight were followed by wet, bare feet quickly climbing up the west bank of the stream. Half an hour later, the girls walked slowly back up the hill, their arms filled with wildflowers. A park ranger politely stopped them in the trail.

"Hello, ladies," he smiled. "Did you miss this somehow?" Leaning over, he placed his hand on a small wooden sign beside the path.

"Wildflowers are protected within state parks. Please leave them for others to enjoy," read Katie aloud. "Oh!" Five young girls lifted stricken eyes and flaming cheeks to the ranger's face. His name was Brad Johnson, according to the shiny metal nametag on his olive green uniform.

"Mr. Johnson," began Katie in a shaky voice, "we didn't even see that sign. Honest, we didn't. I'm so sorry . . ." her voice trailed off as the frightened girls looked at the impressively tall ranger.

"Well girls," he began with a twinkle in his eyes, "you

don't look like the type to ignore signs that you actually did see. I believe you. But please remember in the future that you can't pick flowers in a state park. Okay?" Brad Johnson smiled again as the girls solemnly nodded their heads.

Then Jessica hesitatingly asked, "Would you like us to give these back to you, sir?"

At that, the ranger began laughing. "No, girls. I don't have the patience to glue them back onto the stems, and it wouldn't look any better for me to carry them around than you, now would it? Be sure though," he finished more seriously, "that the rest of your group finds out that no more flowers can be picked. All right?"

"Yes, sir." "We will, sir." "Thank you, Mr. Johnson," several of the girls answered at once.

It was a relieved group of young ladies who walked back up the hill to their families. The girls hurried to place the flowers into their cars, then rejoined the others as the mothers set out food. Beth was sure she would look carefully for signs before she did anything else that day!

In late May, Beth's church held a weekend home mission conference. "What is a home mission?" asked John at the supper table, on the evening before the first meeting.

"Well," Dad began, "you remember hearing us tell you lots of stories about our lives as missionaries in Brazil, don't you?" John nodded, and Dad continued. "We went to Brazil to tell people about Jesus who had never heard of Him. We wanted to let God use us, not only to tell about Him, but also to live out a life before those people that was pleasing to the Lord. That way, they might have an example of what a Christian's life should be like, although we could never do that perfectly.

"A home mission, son, has the same goals as a foreign one, but it is here in the U.S. There are places in this country that have very few Christians, or no Bible-based churches, or an unusual amount of evil. These places need a Christian witness. The speaker tomorrow is a missionary to New York City. New York is a huge place, with many problems and a great deal of wickedness. We call Mr. Erickson a home missionary, because he lives here in our country, instead of in a foreign one. Do you understand?" John nodded again as he took a swallow of milk.

Michael, who sat beside John, added, "Not all home missionaries live in big cities like New York, John. Some live in small towns, or rural areas. There are still many places in the United States that could use a missionary, in spite of the fact that our country was settled by the Pilgrims and their descendants. It really is a shame, when there are whole groups of people in the world who still have no access to Bibles or solid Christian teaching." Michael held a deeper interest in foreign missions, though he was not against home missions. It was, however, a great source of frustration to him that the U.S. had fallen so far as to have a need for home missionaries.

Beth had only half-listened to the conversation so far. Talk about missions, missionaries, furloughs, conferences, and anything else related was quite common at the Grant home. Dad had a real love for the subject, and Mom was always interested too. They both delighted in housing the overnight guests who sometimes visited their church, including missionaries and special speakers.

Now she listened a bit more closely as her father began to tell of the hopes of their church leadership. "If there is enough interest in our church, we would like to join with Grace Church here in town, to send a home missionary somewhere. Each church would commit a certain amount of money every month to support the missionary. We already know of a need brought to our attention by Grace Church. One of their members who moved to Kanesville, Iowa has been unable to find a church with beliefs similar to ours and has requested help in starting a church there. Many people prefer to support home missionaries to more desperate sounding places, like New York or Las Vegas. It seems that the elder/deacon board of Grace Covenant has been praying about supporting a home missionary to Kanesville. Our board has been praying about this, too. We believe it is the Lord's leading. Let's all pray about this — that God's will would be done, if the idea truly is His leading."

Everyone around the table nodded, including Beth. How amazing that a town could have no church like hers! Beth felt sorry for the family who had requested help. How alone they must feel.

The weekend conference seemed to go well. There was plenty of interest aroused in home missions by Mr. Erickson, the missionary to New York. He was a very sincere man, enthusiastic about his work. Beth was inspired by his obvious love for the Lord, and found herself praying earnestly that God would provide the support needed.

Katie was even more excited than Beth. "It would be so nice to see our church have a part in providing that little town of 3,000 with a church like ours. Just think, Beth, girls live there who are our age, and have probably never heard of many of the things we believe. Someone needs to tell them!"

Beth nodded. She hoped that the vote taken Sunday night would see their church help send a home missionary to Kanesville.

And it did. The response was overwhelming, and one of the elders remarked to Dad, "I believe we could send a whole group of missionaries to Iowa, not just one! The Lord has really blessed our efforts."

"He is able to do exceedingly abundantly above all that we ask or think," agreed Dad. "May God receive all the praise for this. It is His mighty work."

Chapter Three

As summer began in earnest, Beth found herself at loose ends a bit. Homeschool activities had stopped for the summer, except for a Bike Day in early June. Once that was past, Beth seldom saw her friends except briefly at church. Katie was busy helping her mother with their huge garden, and all the other work that a large family brought. Beth longed for something to happen, but she was certainly not prepared when something finally did.

At many mealtimes, Michael had spoken of possible plans for the future. He was almost nineteen now, and felt ready to try some mission work. He and Dad seemed to endlessly discuss the different opportunities, and Beth was unhappy every time the subject came up. In fact, after a few minutes, she usually stopped really listening to the conversation.

She and Michael had always been very close, especially in their younger years, though Beth realized that as they had grown older, she had not spent much time with Michael. He was a more quiet and reserved person than she was, content to study, read, and spend time with the family. Beth loved activities, going places, and being with friends. Still, she felt dependent on Michael's presence in their home. Beth didn't want things to change at all. Why did they have to? Why couldn't things just go on as they were?

One evening during supper, the telephone rang. After a few minutes, Dad returned to the table, and addressed Michael excitedly. "That was Bill Parks, Michael. You remember, the director of Hope Unlimited. He has business in Nashville next week and plans to drive all the way over here to see us next weekend. I'm sure we'll be able to discuss with him your hopes of helping out at Hope Unlimited this fall. How about that?" asked Dad, positively beaming.

Beth felt as if her heart had turned over with a sickening flop. Suddenly the seemingly endless discussions that she had refused to listen to were coming to an end. Hope Unlimited was located in Campinas, Brazil, and apparently Dad and Michael had plans that Beth had not been fully aware of.

"This fall? You mean Michael might leave for South America this fall?" Beth's chin quivered and her eyes filled with tears. "So soon? That's only a few months away!" She could no longer hold back the tears, and they quickly spilled over her cheeks. "I don't want Michael to go! I want him here with us! Why does he have to? Why do you **want** to?" she finished, looking at Michael through a film of tears.

Before anyone could answer, Beth jumped up from her chair and ran quickly out the back door. Reaching the safety of the huge willow tree in the backyard, she ducked under its sheltering limbs, just as she had many times as a little girl. She sat there alone under the tree, her back against the trunk, and cried as she had not cried for years. Huge sobs shook her body for several minutes, then finally subsided as she calmed down a little.

Soon the back screen door slammed, and Beth raised her head from her arms to see Michael coming toward the willow. She wondered how he had known where she was. Stooping under the larger limbs, he pushed the long wispy branches aside and entered the large "room" next to the trunk. Silently he seated himself beside Beth and handed her his handkerchief. After a few moments of silence, broken only by the muffled sniffles of his sister, he began to speak quietly.

"I had a feeling this is where you would be. Remember when your kitten died, the year after we moved here? This is where you spent the afternoon that day."

Receiving no response from Beth, he softly continued, "And remember a few years ago, when John and Dad had to

16

be in the hospital for the transplant? The morning Mom took them to St. Mary's, you disappeared. Mrs. Keeley had come to stay with us, and she was so worried. But I knew right where to find you. You know, you used to spend quite a bit of time out here whenever you were upset about something."

Beth had to smile at that, though her smile was a bit weak. Michael paused, then cleared his throat and began to speak again. "Beth, I had no idea this would hit you so hard. Dad and I have been discussing this opportunity, as well as several other ones, for months now. We've brought it up many times at the dinner table. I thought you realized that I would be going somewhere soon. Why, I've talked about going into missions for years. I felt as though God called me to be a missionary when I was a little boy, back when we lived in Brazil. You remember, don't you? How could this be such a shock?"

Beth looked at Michael's kind, sympathetic expression and her eyes filled with tears again. She quickly looked away, then drew a deep, shaky breath. "I guess I knew you wanted to go into foreign missions. I mean, of course I knew you did, but, well, that always seemed to be 'someday.' Someday far away. I didn't know it would come now. I don't want anything to change. I don't want our family to change."

Michael looked thoughtfully at the pattern of leaves and sunlight on the grass before them. "Beth," he began slowly, "we aren't in charge of our lives. If we are Christians, God tells us in the Psalms that we are the sheep of His pasture. Jesus said that He is our Shepherd, and we, as His sheep, know His voice and will follow Him. If He has called me to Brazil, I must follow Him. And you must follow Him too, Beth, wherever He leads you. We can't demand that everything go according to our own human wishes, or that nothing will ever change. That isn't following Him. That isn't any different from the rest of the world."

Silence followed as Beth struggled inwardly. She knew Michael was right. Every word he had spoken was true. Beth felt as though she were standing in a forest, with two paths leading in different directions. One path was familiar, and Beth knew she had always followed it before. It was a path where she did pretty much as she pleased, and she had been happy with that seemingly safe way. The second path led her away from the safe and familiar, away from her own desires. Its course was unknown, as was its end. Michael was going down that passage, ahead of her. Away from her. Was she brave enough to follow the One who stood around the bend of that path, calling her?

Late one hot afternoon in early July, Beth walked into the kitchen to find her mother. Mom, however, was nowhere to be found. Beams of sunlight from the bay window over the sink fell slanting across the shining kitchen floor. The gleaming white countertops were bare, and the stove stood cold and silent. The room had a deserted look, almost as if no one lived in the house. Beth thought that strange, since supper was usually well underway by this time of day. Wandering about the house, she finally found Mom sitting at Dad's desk, with a map and some sheets of paper spread out before her.

"Beth! Did you need something?" Mom hastily shoved the papers aside. Standing up quickly, she came around the desk to the door of the study.

"I just wondered about supper, Mom. It's after five o'clock, and you haven't started anything. Was I supposed to cook tonight and forgot? I didn't remember you asking me to make supper."

"No, dear," smiled Mom. "As a matter of fact, we're doing something pretty special tonight. Dad is taking us out to eat. He said he would be home around 5:30 to pick up the family, so I guess we'd better find the boys. I'm sure they'll

18

need to change to clean clothes before we leave. Would you get the message to them right away, Beth? I'll meet you in front of the house at 5:30." With that, Mom stepped back inside the study and closed the door.

Beth just stood where she was for a minute, staring at the door. The look on her face was "more curious than a cat," as her mother often described it. What was Mom doing? Beth could hear papers rustling on the other side of the closed study door. And why were they going out to eat? The Grant family usually ate out twice a year — once on Mom's birthday, and again on her parents' anniversary. Beth would have stood there trying to figure things out longer, but the clock in the living room caught her attention. It was chiming the quarter hour, and Beth suddenly realized she had only fifteen minutes to find her brothers and change her own clothes. Moving quickly toward the front door, Beth began to get a bit excited. What could be going on?

Forty-five minutes later, Dad asked the blessing at the table in the restaurant. Just moments after he finished, the waitress brought salads, and everyone began eating. Beth noticed that John and Adam didn't seem to be wasting any time on curiosity. They simply seemed glad for another opportunity to eat. Boys.

Then Beth looked across the table at Michael, who merely smiled at Beth and buttered a roll. Beth began to grow just a bit frustrated. She felt uncomfortable asking any questions herself, and her brothers were obviously going to be of no help in finding out anything. She didn't have long to wait, though, before Dad began to speak.

"Isn't anyone going to ask why your wonderful dad decided to take you to this exquisite restaurant for an unbelievably delicious meal tonight?" Dad's face was wearing a broad grin, and Beth could hear excitement in his voice. Mom laughed, and as Beth turned to look at her, she thought Mom looked really excited, too.

Adam answered first. "I don't know why you decided to bring us here, Dad, but I sure am glad you did. Are we going to be allowed to order dessert?"

"Well, I guess that's a pretty typical response from a ten-year-old boy," laughed Dad. "Yes, you'll be allowed to order dessert, Adam. This is a very special night, you see. Mom and I have some really good news we'd like to share with you. We thought this was an excellent way to celebrate the new adventure that we feel God has called us to." He paused for a moment, and Beth tried to comprehend Dad's words. *Celebrate? Adventure? What on earth was going on?*

Dad took a sip of water, then continued. "As you know, Michael will be a missionary in Brazil this fall, at Hope Unlimited. He'll be helping homeless boys to be able to live in a safe place, learn skills, and hear the gospel of Jesus Christ. It's a real answer to prayer for him. Mom and I have received a real answer to prayer, too. You know why we had to move back to the States eight years ago, and we have been so grateful to God for sparing John to us. But we have missed missionary life, and now God has made a way for us to become missionaries again. The elder/deacon board of our church and the board of Grace Church has asked me to become the home missionary to Kanesville, Iowa. Mom and I have spent much time in prayer and discussion about this, as well as in seeking counsel from mature Christian friends. We believe God wants us to accept this call, and we'll be moving to Kanesville about the first week of August."

Beth sat in stunned silence as the boys exploded with questions. The laughter, excited chatter, and general noise seemed to swirl around her. She felt as though her world was upside-down. First Michael leaving, and now this. It was impossible! Surely they wouldn't go! Why, Tennessee was home, not Iowa! What about all her friends? And their church?

Beth could barely remember Brazil. This was home. She was so happy here. Surely, surely they wouldn't really leave. Beth looked up to see her mother's gentle, sympathetic eyes resting on her. The kindness and love there was more than she could bear, and Beth's own eyes filled with tears. Was this the unfamiliar path Jesus was calling her to follow? Was this listening to His voice? Would living a Christian life always mean sorrow-filled goodbyes?

Chapter Four

The following week found the Grant family in Kanesville for a few days. Dad and Mom needed to find a house to live in, and Beth's church was also praying that a small building could be found, so that the new church could be started right away.

There wasn't much choice in the way of housing. Kanesville was very small, and was set in the midst of corn and pig farms. John and Adam hoped for a house in the country, but Dad felt that God wanted them in town. That way the Grants could meet people more easily and frequently, as well as being seen as part of the community.

Beth, becoming ever more discouraged, walked through the few houses for sale with her parents. This was certainly nothing like home. "Home" was a fairly new brick house, in a modern subdivision, with a landscaped yard and wide streets. Kanesville looked nothing like what Beth was used to. It had narrow streets, broken sidewalks, and older white frame houses, most of which had sagging wooden steps leading to sagging wooden porches.

Mom loved the old-fashioned looking homes, and was really excited about one in particular. She kept trying to interest Beth in thinking of how the house would look with new paint and steps, old-fashioned lace curtains, and new wallpaper.

All Beth could seem to focus on were things like doors that either got stuck easily or wouldn't close at all, the narrow squeaky steps leading to the small bedrooms upstairs, and the worn linoleum in the kitchen. She sighed as the Grants went back through her mother's favorite house the third time. This must be the one Dad had decided to buy. Well, it wasn't any worse than any of the others. In fact, it was the one Beth liked best, if she had to choose one. But she wasn't about to admit it. She dreaded moving from their large beautiful house into this old smaller one. She would simply try not to think about it until she had to.

The only enjoyable event of the week for Beth was meeting the Newman family. Stephen and Christine Newman had three small children, and they were the family that had requested a home missionary three years before. Stephen was the manager of the only large grocery store in town. He was a young man, with a quick laugh and an abundance of energy. He seemed to do everything fast, and Beth wondered if that had helped him to get the job he had, or if his job had helped him become fast at everything he did. His wife Christine was sweet and shy, with a gentle smile and soft voice. She was very patient with their children, who were quick to win Beth's affections. Joshua was five, Matthew was three, and little Lydia had just had her first birthday.

Beth never tired of watching the little boys play with their younger sister. She had never seen boys so young be that gentle with a baby. Watching the Newman children brought thoughts of Katie's family, and the fact that she would be moving far away from the Myers just two weeks from now. How could she bear it?

Soon after Beth arrived back in Tennessee, she found an opportunity to spend an afternoon with Katie Myers. The girls sat in Katie's kitchen, talking as they baked cookies. Katie's brothers kept coming in to see if any cookies were ready, so they didn't really have any time for private conversation until a couple of batches had come out of the oven. Mrs. Myers allowed the boys a few cookies apiece, then shooed them outside to eat, leaving the girls finally alone.

"How was the trip to Iowa, Beth? Did you find a place to live? What is Kanesville like?" Katie's questions tumbled out one after another, as she placed a third pan full of cookies into the oven. Her voice was cheerful and excited, and Beth was a bit hurt. Didn't Katie realize Beth was going to live there permanently? That they couldn't see each other, or go to homeschool activities together anymore? How could Katie be so enthusiastic?

"Well," Beth slowly began, "we did find a house. And Mom and Dad and the boys enjoyed the trip. But, oh Katie, it's just awful! The town is little and old, and the house is old. There are no mountains, and the countryside is flat and bare. Just cornfields and pig farms and hardly any trees. There won't be anything fun to do. The Newmans are nice, but they have only little children, and they don't know of anyone in town that homeschools! There aren't any shopping centers or malls — just an old-fashioned square with a few little stores. And of course, there's no church like ours, except the one Dad will be starting. All my friends will be here. I'll be so lonely — especially without you, Katie."

Beth had been fighting back tears, and now she couldn't keep them from falling. "I feel as though I can't bear to go, but I have no choice. I have to! What will I do?" she exclaimed, looking at Katie's sober face.

Katie was silent. The timer went off on the oven. She pulled out the finished cookies, slid in another pan, then re-set the timer before she answered. "Beth, I'm so sorry you feel this way. I knew you would miss the church and everything, but I had no idea you would be so unhappy. I've been excited for you, and sort of wishing it was our family that God had called to be missionaries to Kanesville."

Beth stared at her friend in disbelief. "You've been wishing your family could move? Why? Don't you see how awful it's going to be?" Beth's expression clearly added the idea — and don't you feel sorry for me?"

Katie sat back down and looked seriously into Beth's eyes. "I'm truly sorry it's so hard for you, Beth. But you know, something you said a moment ago is not really true. You said all your friends are here. But they aren't all going to be here. You're taking your closest friends with you — your family. You won't be alone, Beth. You and your Mom and Dad and brothers will be together. It seems like an adventure! I know there are some things you don't like, but if God has called you, He will give you good things there, too."

"God called Mom and Dad. I never felt like He called me," Beth returned. "Why should I be happy about something I never wanted?"

"But God **has** called you, Beth," Katie answered. "You are part of your family, and if God has called your dad, and you are still at home, unmarried, under his authority and protection, then God has called you, too. It's a privilege, Beth! You'll get to help that little town learn about how people live who believe the Bible is truth. You'll be a real missionary! And I know God is going to help you be happy there. That is, if you really want to be happy, and if you ask Him to help you."

Katie's words stung Beth. *If you really want to be happy? How could you say that?* thought Beth. Looking into Katie's sweet face though, Beth felt the sting subside quickly. Katie had not meant to hurt her. Katie truly was her best friend, and only wanted to help. But why couldn't she understand?

Beth lay awake a long time that night. She turned Katie's words over in her mind again and again. Katie had said that Beth would be taking her best friends with her — her family. But were they truly her best friends? Beth suddenly realized that although she had always thought of Katie as her best friend, and had often spoken of her as being her best friend, she had never heard Katie say the same. Katie obviously enjoyed Beth's company, but the friendship did not seem to be quite so important to Katie as it was to Beth. Was it because Katie was more content with her own family? Were they really her best friends?

Beth's eyes felt hot, staring at the ceiling in the darkness. Was God using this move to teach her to be less dependent on her friends? There would be no homeschool group, no activities. No like-minded girls her age — at least, not that she was aware of. Beth felt all her props being pulled out from under her. Would she fall? She had always thought she was committed to God, and His ways. Had she been simply committed to her own ways, with Him tacked on as an afterthought? Beth had become very confused in the past few weeks. Tossing and turning late into the night, Beth again gave way to tears.

Chapter Five

The first week of August brought heat and humidity to Kanesville. As the moving truck backed into the tree-lined driveway at 1209 Lincoln Avenue, Beth thanked the Lord for the blessings He had provided. She reflected this morning that the tall, stately trees shading the yard and house afforded much in the way of relief from the heat. Perhaps this old neighborhood, with the large lots and abundance of full-grown shade trees, would prove to have some advantages over a more modern one after all.

Beth stood at the side of the wooden porch, leaning against the tall corner post. The driver slowly maneuvered the truck as close as possible to the small covered stoop outside the kitchen door. That truck contained all the familiar possessions that would, hopefully, transform this old house into some semblance of home.

At least, she reflected with an attempt at a smile, she would have a bed to sleep in again. Old wooden floors lacked something in comparison to carpet, for comfort in sleeping anyway. Of course, Mom would never admit that. She loved old wooden floors as much as she loved old wooden houses with peeling paint and squeaky doors.

With an effort, Beth turned her thoughts to the business at hand. She had promised the Lord last night that she truly would try to be cheerful and happy today. Briefly closing her eyes, she rested her forehead against the peeling corner porch post and asked His help again in fulfilling that promise. Making herself smile, she headed back into the house to ask Mom what needed to be done.

"There you are, Beth!" Mom greeted her daughter

cheerfully, then smiled as she reached over and removed a small fragment of white paint from Beth's forehead. Even Beth had to laugh.

Michael had promised to help Dad fix the porch steps, paint the house, and do innumerable other repair jobs in the few weeks remaining before he left for his mission field. Adam and John would be helping also, and Dad was sure that they could accomplish quite a bit. For now though, the furniture on the truck had to be coaxed into the smaller rooms of their new house.

Beth began rolling up sleeping bags, moving suitcases, and trying to clear as much floor space as possible. The men from the truck grunted and strained in the still morning air as the day continued to warm. Mom had every window open, and the shade trees outside did their best, but Beth was already missing the convenience of modern air-conditioning.

"Don't worry, honey," smiled Dad, as she unintentionally complained of the heat. The Grants had stopped for a break to eat some cheese, crackers, and fruit. It did feel cooler on the porch at least, and there really was a slight breeze there. "We'll have a cooler house when we find the fans. Years ago that was the only air-conditioning we had. Wait and see. When the men finish with unloading, and we get some air moving in the house, it will be much cooler."

Late in the afternoon, it truthfully was cooler in the house. The men had finally gone, and the furniture was in place "at least for now," teased Mom. The boys and Dad gave exaggerated groans. Everyone knew how much Mom loved to direct the frequent rearrangement of furniture. She always said it made her feel as though she had a new house.

The whole family sat down to rest a few minutes in the living room. Unpacked boxes stood amidst the furniture, and there were no curtains, pictures, or other small homey touches to be seen. Yet Beth felt more grateful to the Lord than she had felt for several weeks. He had answered her prayer today, so completely. Except for the accidental complaint about the heat at lunch, Beth had remained cheerful all day.

Looking around the room now, she quietly studied each of her family members. She was thankful and glad to have them with her. They really were her friends. But Beth realized that it would take much effort on her part, as well as God's blessing and help, to make them her best friends. She had wasted far too much time on unimportant things in the past, and now she felt a real urgency to start fresh with her family. She silently asked the Lord to help her tomorrow as He had today, and to teach her how to truly love each one.

Work on the house did progress quite rapidly, once all the boxes were unpacked and the house was settled — "for now, at least," Mom reminded them all. Dad replaced the linoleum in the kitchen and installed a new bathroom sink, while the boys painted every room in the house. Later they would begin painting kitchen cabinets, and replacing some of the light fixtures. Scraping and painting the outside of the house was put off until the weather should cool down a bit, in September.

"I never knew you were so good at this!" exclaimed Beth. She was viewing the bathroom for the first time with its new paint and sink.

Dad laughed, "Missionaries often have to be their own carpenters and plumbers! I used to do quite a bit of this years ago. The larger church in Tennessee kept me too busy for much handyman work around the house there. Too, it was a much newer house, and didn't need much help." He put his arm around Beth and gave her a hug. "I'm kind of glad this old house needs some help. It fills up some time and makes me feel I'm making progress on something."

Beth gave her dad a smile and hugged him back, resolving to pray for him more. She knew he was a little discouraged about the fact that no one had shown any real interest yet in the church. Their second week in Iowa, Dad had spent a couple of hours a day trying to meet people. He walked around the courthouse square, browsed in shops, and walked through the neighborhoods in town. At the end of the week, the Newman family had asked the Grants over for supper. During the meal, Stephen had spoken to Dad about the necessity of not moving too fast.

"The people here are likely different from the people you are used to dealing with. This is a small town and Iowans are a bit more reserved. At least, they seem so to me," Stephen added. "They don't make decisions fast, and they usually are pretty set in their ways. Try going a little slower, and give them time to get to know you. They'll have to learn that you are an honest person, not some hypocrite, before they'll want to even consider visiting your church."

So Dad had tried to slow down and simply go on with work on the house. Those first three weeks saw only the Newmans and Grants worshiping together at the Grant home on Sunday morning. But the first week of September brought encouraging changes. Stephen seemed to know almost everyone in town by name, since most people bought groceries in the store he managed. He began to mention to people that Dad was hoping to find a small building to purchase for a new church. As word got around town, an elderly man approached Stephen at the store one Monday.

"Hear that new preacher's looking to buy a place," remarked Mr. Thurman loudly. "I got me a little building that was once the old elementary school, years back. Don't know why they ever replaced that old schoolhouse. Was good enough for my kids." Mr. Thurman blew his nose loudly into his handkerchief, cleared his throat noisily a few times, then continued. "I don't have no use for it, but I couldn't stand to see it torn down, it being perfectly good. I only paid $500 for it forty year ago. I reckon I'd take $4,000 for it now. You tell that new preacher about James Thurman having a building and see if he wants to take him a look. I'll leave it unlocked this week, and he can go see it. It's a street over from the feed store, beside the old railroad track. You know where it is."

"Thanks, Mr. Thurman!" Stephen Newman exclaimed. "I'm sure Mr. Grant will be glad to hear of it."

As he put his battered cap back on his head, the elderly Mr. Thurman replied, "Yep," and left the store.

Mom, Dad, Beth, and Stephen Newman went to see Mr. Thurman's old schoolhouse early Tuesday morning. Set between two large scraggly trees in a yard of overgrown weeds, the schoolhouse certainly didn't look very promising to Beth. She couldn't believe someone would actually think Dad would consider buying it for a church. *It's so tiny*, she thought, *and it would take so much work. You couldn't put many people in there at all! And what about rooms for offices and meetings? This building isn't even a possibility,* her thoughts continued as they opened the front door.

Inside the little frame building were just two rooms. The larger room had a few old wooden desks and parts of desks, scattered about on the floor. Cobwebs were hanging from the light fixtures, a thick carpet of white dust covered the floor, and mouse-chewed books lay stacked in one corner. The smaller room had rows of old-fashioned coat hooks, a few rickety small tables, and an ancient rusty sink at one end. The floor was littered with torn maps and pieces of blackboard. Bright fall sunshine struggled through the dirt-streaked windows, and a musty smell pervaded the air.

"Oh!" exclaimed Mrs. Grant, and Beth quickly turned to her mother, expecting that she had tripped over something on the floor. But Betty Grant was standing, hands clasped in front of her, eyes shining. "Isn't it just too good to be true?"

she exclaimed, looking happily at Beth's father. "Robert, the Lord is truly providing for us here. This is so exciting."

Beth sighed inaudibly. She should have known. Mom loved anything old-fashioned, absolutely anything. But Dad wasn't an antique nut. He had a very common-sense outlook on life, for which Beth was especially grateful in a situation like this.

"It sure does look as though He prepared our way," Dad agreed. "This is a real answer to prayer. Let's take a look around outside, Stephen. Wonder if the foundation is still sound?" He and Mr. Newman walked out the back door of the building, and Beth stood transfixed, unable to believe what she had just heard.

Seeing the expression on Beth's face, Mom began laughing, and gave her daughter's shoulders a hug. As if she could read Beth's mind, she said, "What did you expect, honey? This is a small town, and so far we have a total of eleven people in the church. Even if it grows, there are only 3,000 people in the whole town. Beth, there were 60,000 people in the last town we lived in. That's twenty times more! Think of our church in Tennessee, and cut the number of people by 95%. Cut the money by 95%. Don't you think this building is just about right?"

Beth looked at her mother soberly. "I don't know, Mom. I guess so." She was no longer incredulous, just resigned. It was surely different here, and the sooner she could stop thinking about the way things had been back home, the better off she would probably be.

In addition to providing a building for the new church, God supplied another change in circumstances that first week of September. An older couple stopped by the Grant home Saturday evening as the family sat on the front porch. Mr. and Mrs. Jensen introduced themselves, and sat down for a little while when Dad offered them chairs. Beth remembered seeing the couple walk by every evening, and the Jensens told the Grants that they lived just two blocks further east on Lincoln Avenue.

Before the half-hour visit was over, Dad had told them about the new church, and the Jensens had decided to join the Grants and Newmans for worship on Sunday morning. That was the beginning of a wonderful friendship between the three families.

Sadie Jensen was a very sweet and soft-spoken woman, and she reminded Beth of Grandmother Grant. She seemed to truly fit the ideal of an older Christian woman. Each time Beth saw her, she was reminded of the words she and her mother had read together from the book of Titus — "as becometh holiness."

Carl Jensen was a tall, thin man, who seemed much too full of energy for seventy-five years of age. He volunteered to spend much time working on the old schoolhouse over the next few months, getting it cleaned up and repaired for use. Beth began to feel a bit of her parents' excitement about the church. Who would God send next to their little fellowship?

The third week of September arrived, and with it came the departure date for Michael. Michael had shown only excitement about going to Brazil, at least until just before leaving for the airport. Since Des Moines was over three hours away from Kanesville, the Grants planned to leave soon after breakfast for Michael to catch his plane. At breakfast, Dad asked a special blessing on Michael, requesting God's provision and safe-keeping on his oldest son for the next ten months. After the "amen," Michael's head remained bowed for several moments.

Then, eyes filled with tears, he looked around the table at them all. "Keep me in your prayers each day, please," he requested in a shaky voice that didn't sound quite like Michael's. "It will be so good to know that you are all here together, praying for me." With that, he left the room for several minutes, but when he came back, he was smiling and cheerful again. While he had been out of the room, several other family members had hunted for a handkerchief, or cleared their throats quite a bit. But throughout the rest of the morning, everyone remained cheerful and calm.

Driving home from the airport, Dad explained more about the City of Youth, operated by Hope Unlimited, to Adam and John. "It's located in Campinas, which is about 300 miles west of Rio de Janeiro, Brazil. Michael is going to help teach homeless boys there. They need to learn skills to be able to earn a living, but they need most of all to hear about Jesus. These boys have been living on the streets, usually stealing and begging to get enough food to survive. Their lives are often in danger from angry storekeepers and other citizens. Hope Unlimited takes these boys to a camp, called the City of Youth, where they are provided with warm beds and good food. People like Michael teach them about Jesus, and help them learn to read the Bible. The boys are then trained for a trade like electrical installation, carpentry, metal work, civil construction, and auto mechanics. They are guaranteed to find a job when they complete their training program. God has used Hope Unlimited to help many boys become Christians, and to find an entirely new life."

"How old are the boys, Dad? Are they older than me?" asked John.

"Some are younger and some are older," replied Dad. "Most are there for several years."

"How about girls?" asked Beth. "Is there a place in Brazil for homeless girls?"

"Hope Unlimited is starting a work there for girls," answered her father. "As we pray for Michael and the boys at the City of Youth, let's remember the girls' needs, too."

Chapter Six

The fall and winter passed slowly for Beth, in spite of plenty of work to be done. In addition to her studies, Beth helped with homeschooling her younger brothers. She began checking some of their work, to save Mom time, and Mom responded by teaching Beth to sew — a skill Beth now realized she should have mastered long ago.

One March evening, as she began ripping out a seam she had sewn wrong sides together, Beth sighed loudly. "When will I ever do it right?" she complained to Mom. "It seems I am forever making mistakes. It takes me so long to finish just a simple skirt. You are so much faster than I am," she finished with a note of discouragement in her voice.

"I should hope so!" her mother cheerfully replied. "If I had not become better and faster at sewing over a period of twenty years, it would be a sorry state of affairs. You have to remember that I made just as many mistakes when I was learning to sew, and I still make them, you know. Why do you suppose I own two seam rippers?" she added with a smile. "It's because I am always misplacing one somewhere, and I still use them quite often! Does that help you any?"

"A little," Beth admitted. "If you think I can someday be as good and fast a seamstress as you are, I guess it will be worth it to keep trying."

"That's more like it," approved Mom. "And you're getting a head start on me, Beth. You're only seventeen. I didn't learn to sew until I was expecting Michael. You will have much more time and energy to devote to learning now, without a young baby to care for."

Beth ripped for a few minutes in silence. Pausing, she

looked over at Mom, who was writing letters at Dad's desk in the corner. "Maybe there are some other things I should start learning, Mom," she said. "If God lets me be a wife and mother someday, it would be easier to learn things now, like you said. But what else should I be learning? I mean, besides cooking," she added hastily.

Mom looked up and smiled at that. Beth was learning many new cooking skills this year, and had asked for a short break from it this week. After three failed batches of bread in a row, she had become frustrated, and Mom had agreed to let her try again after a few days respite.

"Well," Mom began, "Dad and I garden every year. And we had hoped to grow a really big one this coming summer. You have helped weed in the past, even though it was forced labor! How about this year taking a real interest in it? You can help order seeds, plan where everything should be planted, and learn how to care for all the different kinds of vegetables and fruits."

"Okay," Beth agreed a bit doubtfully. "But how hard could that be? I mean, you just make rows and plant the seeds, then weed the plants when they come up. And gather the harvest at the end of summer. There isn't really much to learn, is there?"

"You'd be surprised," Mom replied. "I'm still learning, and I have gardened for twenty years. I began the same year that I began sewing. There is always something to learn, every gardening season. And Beth," Mom continued, "you'll find out this very first year that there is much more to gardening than just planting seeds. You have to think of how tall the different plants grow, so that they won't shade each other. You have to allow different amounts of space for each one also — a stalk of corn takes up much more room than a carrot. And some plants grow best when planted next to certain other plants — that's called companion planting. All of these things have to be planned out ahead of time. There are also decisions to be made about how much to plant of each thing you grow. If you plan to store food for winter, or do any canning, you need to plant much more."

Mom paused and smiled at Beth, eyes sparkling. "Why, I'm getting excited just thinking about it. Dad and I had only small gardens the last few years in Tennessee. I haven't really tried to grow most of our food for a long time. This will be fun — but hard work, too," she added.

"If it's such hard work to grow a really big garden, why should you?" asked Beth. "I don't mean to sound lazy, but we do just fine buying things at the store, don't we?" she finished, a bit embarrassed.

Mom came over to the couch and sat down beside Beth. "Honey, it's true that we can get along with things from the store. But just because we can buy things from a store, doesn't mean that we should. There are several good reasons that I think everyone should know how to raise their own food."

"First," began Mom, "it saves lots of money. Raising your own food is really much cheaper than buying it at the store, especially if you don't feel that you need lots of expensive gadgets or store-bought fertilizer. If you pay less for your food, you have more money to give to others who are in need. Homegrown food is also much better for you. Produce from grocery stores usually has been sprayed with dangerous chemicals. In addition, the produce has often been shipped from far away, and food loses some of its nutrition after a few days of storage."

Mom settled back comfortably into a corner of the couch. "And now I am going to explain another reason to you, Beth. Your dad and I feel very strongly about this, probably because of the years we spent on the missionary field. You see, we couldn't depend on grocery stores in Brazil. We had to grow much of our food ourselves, or not eat. You probably remember pulling some weeds in our garden there. Of course, there was a small market in the village, and a few times a year we would make a trip to Belem to buy some things. But we really needed to know how to raise our basic food ourselves, depending only on God to bless our efforts, not on other people to supply our daily needs.

"Unfortunately, once we were back in the States for a few years, we began to fall back into old habits, and to buy more and more of our food, only raising a small amount. The fact is, that although many people depend on American grocery stores to supply their food, they may not always be able to do so. God has provided for those people in this way in the past. And He may continue to in the future. But then again, He may not."

"Our lives and daily food depend on His blessing alone. Growing their own food seems to make that more a reality for most people. We need to be sure we are really depending on God to provide for us, and not just taking our food for granted. "

"I see, Mom," Beth spoke thoughtfully. "I really do want to help this year, and learn all I can. If God ever calls me to some place where I need to raise my food, I'd like to already have lots of experience. But we can't learn to do everything ourselves, can we? I mean, what about when John was a baby and got so sick? You had to have help from a hospital. You couldn't have saved his life by yourself. So how do we know how much to depend on others' help?"

"That's a really good question, Beth, and I don't have a really good answer," Mom replied. "We certainly did need help for John, and we were very grateful for it. Of course, the doctors couldn't have saved John unless it was God's will, no matter how skilled or knowledgeable they were. They were His instruments. And no, we didn't do everything for our-

38

selves in South America. We didn't make our own shoes, or weave our own fabric." Mom smiled. "Still, I think that we need to avoid the view of life that expects everything to simply be handed to us, without any work at all. God tells us in I Thessalonians to work with our own hands, that we may have lack of nothing. Each of us needs to pray, and ask God what we need to be doing. I'm sure it won't be exactly the same for everyone, since He is the one who places us in different circumstances. But remember," Mom added, "He tells us in I Timothy that He doesn't want us to be lazy, wandering about from house to house!"

"I remember," smiled Beth. "And I'll try hard to learn to work with my hands this year. Learning to be a keeper at home and to guide the house isn't as simple as I thought it would be!"

Mom laughed, then added, "And just wait until God adds children into the picture. That can really be a challenge if you've had no experience. Now, where can we find some children for you to practice on?"

Mom's question was answered in early April, when Stephen and Christine Newman's fourth child was born. The baby was in a difficult breech position, making a C-section necessary, much to Christine's dismay. She soon accepted the situation as God's will, however, and regained her usual cheerful spirit.

A few days after little Faith Christine's birth, Christine came home with doctor's orders for plenty of rest and no heavy lifting. For the next several weeks, Beth spent two or three hours every morning at the Newman home. Each morning Joshua and Matthew greeted her with excited little voices, and even Lydia chimed in with "Bef! Bef!" Beth enjoyed caring for the children, cleaning the house, and even doing the laundry, which had never been a favorite chore.

Before Beth left for the day, she made sure she had some preparations for supper already underway. Both Christine and Stephen were grateful for her help, and Beth found it a real pleasure to be needed.

Those were very instructive and valuable hours for Beth. She had a chance to observe Christine closely for long periods of time, and she was impressed again with how patient and gentle Christine was with her children. Christine never raised her voice, yet her children almost always obeyed her quickly. It was altogether a wonderful experience for Beth — one that she was to remember years later, when she had children of her own.

The month of May brought many pleasant surprises for the Grant family. Grace Mission, as the little church was called, reached a total of thirty-five regular attenders. This was such an encouragement to Beth's father. Dad felt as though God was reassuring him that He had indeed called the Grants as missionaries to Kanesville. Among the new people attending Grace Mission was the Cooper family. Frank and Pam Cooper had two daughters, one a year older than Beth, and one a year younger. Beth was hopeful that the girls would share her ideals, but those hopes were soon forgotten.

Amy and Cindy were very involved with dating, parties, and cheerleading. They were quite friendly toward Beth, although she only saw them at church on Sundays. Beth prayed that the Lord would use her in some way to encourage the girls in their Christian walk.

Early May also brought previously hidden surprises to the yard on Lincoln Avenue. Tulips appeared in bright clusters along the driveway, and lovely pink blossoms covered a small crabapple tree outside the kitchen window. A few weeks later, two large bushes in a corner of the yard bloomed into fragrant lilacs, and Beth had to admit that even Iowa was beautiful in the spring.

June found Beth immersed in garden work. Mom had been right. There was quite a bit more to raising a large garden than Beth had previously thought. Much time was spent in weeding, thinning, and bug patrol. Bugs — ugh! Mom believed in picking the garden pests off the plants rather than spraying. Beth was overjoyed when she walked into the garden early one morning and found Adam and John busily filling quart jars with potato bugs.

"Mom said she'd pay us a penny a bug!" exclaimed John in excitement. "Plus, we're going to have a huge supply of food for George and Martha."

Beth was puzzled for a moment, before she remembered that George and Martha were Adam and John's newest pet frogs. "That's great, guys," she agreed. "And thanks, Mom," Beth added as her mother walked over from the flower bed to join them.

"You're welcome, sweetheart," Mom smiled. "I decided we shouldn't be selfish and have all the fun ourselves, when the boys would enjoy the job so much!"

The boys had already found many things to enjoy about their new home. The yard was much larger than their old one had been. The trees were mature, so there were many places ideal for tree-houses or forts. The shady lot ran far back behind the house, with a gentle slope down to the creek. Plenty of small creatures inhabited the banks, including the frogs that had kept Beth awake the first few nights. She was used to the noise now, but she was not used to Adam and John's enthusiasm for their new pets. They seemed to be always introducing Beth to another long-legged green friend, and Beth tried her best to seem interested, instead of nervous. Thankfully, Mom was not fond of frogs herself, and had definite rules about where they were and were not allowed.

Besides the vegetable garden, Beth and Mom had planted several varieties of flowers around the yard. Beth realized one day that the old white house had really begun to look quite pretty, in spite of her former opinions. A large bed of impatiens was planted along the edge of the front porch, making a warm contrast to the cool white paint. On either side of the sunny walk that led to the shady porch, Mom had planted pansies. The tall shade trees along the driveway and around the house were once again providing a welcome relief from the summer heat. Beth found herself thinking of Kanesville as "home," more and more.

Except for the occasional letters from Katie Myers, Beth seldom heard from any of her friends in Tennessee. At first the letters had been frequent from the girls, but as time went on, the correspondence became a trickle. The mailbox did hold other letters for her, however. For Beth's seventeenth birthday in January, Katie had subscribed to a girl's magazine as a gift for her. The magazine was published by two homeschooling girls who wanted to encourage other Christian young ladies, and Beth found much enjoyment in the pages.

That magazine eventually led her to two others, very similar to the first. Many girls wrote to these magazines, some requesting pen-pals. Beth decided to write to a few whose interests and ages were close to her own, and was now writing to five girls on a regular basis, besides Katie. What a blessing it was for Beth to have frequent communication with these girls. She found herself encouraged to live in a closer relationship with her Savior. A deeper commitment to many of her values began to take place in Beth's heart. Two of her pen-pals in particular seemed to always write letters that called Beth to a more committed life.

She slowly began to recognize the fact that there were many girls in situations much like her own. Some were isolated from other Christian friends by distance, and some felt isolated by their standards. Beth was thinking of this late one evening as she sat at Dad's desk. She had been answering a letter from one of her favorite pen-pals, Jeannie, and had paused for a moment. Gazing absently out the window, she watched the moonlight in the yard creating shifting shadows on the grass, as the leaves of the trees moved with a soft breeze. She spent quite some time in her silent reverie, before she was brought back to the living room by her mother's voice.

"Beth? Do you know how late it is?" Mom's soft whisper from the steps made Beth take a quick look at the clock. She was surprised to see that it was almost eleven. No wonder the house had grown so quiet!

"I'm sorry, Mom," Beth apologized as Mom appeared at the bottom of the steps. "I was trying to finish a letter, and I guess my thoughts ran away with me. I had no idea I had been sitting here so long. I'll finish tomorrow." Beth began to quietly gather her things as Mom watched.

"You aren't worried about anything, are you Beth?" Mom questioned her daughter as she began turning off the lights in the room.

"Oh no, Mom," Beth replied reassuringly as she paused, one hand on the lamp on Dad's desk. "As a matter of fact, I was just thinking of all the girls who are in situations like mine — you know, kind of alone." Hastily Beth added, "Not that I'm truly alone. I have you and Dad, and Adam and John. And the Newmans and the Jensens . . . and I have the Lord."

Beth was silent a moment, then continued, "But I have no girls my age who live near me, who are anything like me. Amy and Cindy are friendly, but we certainly don't have much in common. I had just been sitting here thinking about the girls that I correspond with, and so many other girls that I read about in my new magazines. There are lots of us who have no close fellowship with others like us. I'm not alone in my aloneness. Do you know what I mean, Mom?"

"I think so," nodded her mother. "You know Beth, God

gave us an example to follow in His Son, Jesus Christ. Jesus had been in heaven, immortal, the Creator of the world. 'All things were made by Him, and without Him was not anything made that was made.' When He came to earth, He left behind all those who knew Him as He truly was — His Father, and the angels. Imagine how lonely He may have felt at times. Yet He was willing to suffer loneliness in order to accomplish the Father's will, and to glorify the Father. Our loneliness can also be used to accomplish God's will, and to glorify Him, if we have the right attitude. 'Not my will, but Thine be done.' We should remember that God will supply our needs, even our need for fellowship, if it truly is a need. For now, He is supplying your need through pen-pals, magazines, and those of us who live right here with you. That's more than some people have."

"Yes, Mom," Beth agreed softly. "And I'm just beginning to realize how good God is to me, to give me all the encouragement that He has. I'll pray for those other girls as well."

Chapter Seven

$\mathcal{B}$eth glanced at the clock on the wall again. 11:07. Only ten minutes to wait now, if the plane was on schedule. She hoped the next ten minutes would go faster than the first ten had. How could the hands on the clock move so slowly?

Joining Adam and John at the window, Beth watched the activity below her. Men wearing headphones were everywhere, driving luggage trams, trucks, moving equipment — all very fast. "Neat!" exclaimed John. "I'd love to do that, wouldn't you?"

"Boy, can you believe they get paid for that job?" added Adam.

Beth smiled to herself. She wondered if those men below had watched at a window years ago, and were now living out their boyhood wishes. That would help explain the speed at which they were driving!

The clock was forgotten as she watched the men, and Beth was surprised when Adam exclaimed, "It's here! That must be Michael's plane! Look, John!" A large plane was taxiing up to the gate just in front of her, and she squinted against the sudden glare of sunlight as the plane turned. Hoping to get a glimpse of a familiar face at one of the airplane's windows, Beth tried shading her eyes, but the sunshine reflected on the plane was just too strong. She joined her parents near the door for deplaning passengers and tried to wait patiently.

As passengers began to walk past the Grants, her eyes followed an older couple whose arms were filled with packages. Behind her, Beth could hear several excited little voices. "Grandma! Grandma!" "Hi, Grandpa!" "Here we are!" Turning, Beth saw three young children with a homemade sign of blue cardboard, the words "Welcome Grandma and Grandpa" crookedly lettered at the top. Underneath were small pictures of hearts, flowers, rainbows, and unidentifiable animals.

Beth's eyes suddenly filled with tears, as she remembered just such a sign that she had once helped hold for Grandmother Grant. That had been many years ago, but the memory seemed especially clear and sweet to Beth. She would never have the opportunity to welcome Grandmother to their home again, and it was hard to get used to the idea. Just last week Grandmother had gone to be with the Lord, only a few months after being diagnosed with cancer. Michael didn't even know yet.

"There he is!" Mrs. Grant's voice sounded happy but shaky, and she reached for her son even before he could get close enough to touch. Hugs, laughter, tears, and smiles mingled together as they all greeted Michael.

How brown and strong he looked! Beth could hardly believe it was the same Michael who had left in September. Had he been that tall? And his hair — how different it looked! Michael had written that he and his fellow workers gave each other haircuts — maybe they needed some lessons! But Michael had never looked so dear to Beth.

After collecting Michael's luggage, the family drove to a nearby restaurant. As Beth looked around the table at her family, memories of another restaurant meal a year before came flooding back. It was almost frightening, the changes that could occur in just one year. What changes would the next year bring?

Driving home that afternoon, Michael began listing all of the foods he had missed while he was in Brazil. "Mom, could you make Swiss steak sometime soon?" he requested.

"Of course!" exclaimed his mother, delighted that he had missed her cooking. "I'll be glad to make anything you like.

Just name it."

With a broad grin, Michael complied. "German chocolate cake, baked apples, ham, fried chicken, potato salad, carrot cake, banana pudding, biscuits with honey, and cherry cheesecake. That's just a start, of course. Let me think for a while, and I'm sure I can come up with a few more." Turning to John and Adam, he yawned. "I'll need complete and absolute silence for a little while guys, so I can concentrate on that list. After all, you'll get to enjoy the results as much as I will!" With that, Michael leaned his head back and closed his eyes.

The Grant family sat together on the porch once again that evening. "How I've missed this," Michael quietly remarked. "I feel so 'home.'"

"Were you homesick in Brazil?" questioned Adam. "We missed you, but I didn't know you missed us."

"Yes, I missed you all, Adam," answered Michael. "Especially the first few weeks. I enjoy working with the boys there and I know God wants me to continue the work. I'm sure I'll even be glad to go back in September. But you know, I had a lot of adjustments to make when I left home, and I really did feel homesick occasionally."

"What kind of adjustments did you have to make?" asked Beth curiously. "Is the food really different? Did you get sick from the water?"

Michael smiled over at Mom, who sat beside him on the new porch swing. "The food was definitely not Mom's great cooking. We had plenty to eat of nourishing food, but I missed the flavor of home!"

"I guess one of the biggest adjustments was working so closely with strangers. The other workers aren't strangers now, of course, but they certainly were when I arrived. The men that I work with are dedicated Christians, and I have a great deal of respect for them all. But even so, people are real, if you know what I mean. They have individual personalities, individual strengths and weaknesses. I had been used to being around just my family. Occasionally I spent time with a few friends, but only when I wanted to spend time with them. At the City of Youth, I have to be around people who are not members of my family all day long. I have to be patient with boys who have lived very difficult lives, and who don't have the same values I do. I have to live a very consistent life, whether I feel like it or not, because those boys are watching — always watching."

Michael leaned forward, his voice serious. "You know, I found that it is one thing to profess to be a follower of Jesus Christ, and another to make that profession true in your life, day after day. There really isn't any vacation from it — no time off. And, no way to do it without the Lord's help."

The family sat in silence for several minutes before the questions began again. As Michael related more of his life in South America, the hour grew late. At last Dad looked at his watch. "Time for bed, guys," he told Adam and John. "You'll need to start mowing the lawn early tomorrow morning, before it gets too hot. I'm sure the rest of us will be in soon."

After Michael had departed once again for Brazil, Beth found herself growing discontented again. How could she grow discontented? With Michael home, she had been quite happy. Beth had felt that all her inward struggles were behind her. But now all the old feelings she thought she had buried in the past year seemed to rise back to the surface of her mind. She tried scolding herself for focusing on the past, yet often let her mind wander back to Tennessee, her old friends, and the church in which she had been so happy. She knew she was being unwise to let herself dwell on her own desires, and that it was displeasing to God, but she felt helpless to change.

On a cold Saturday afternoon in November, Beth decided to go to her father for help. His sermon the previous Sunday had been based upon Philippians 4:4-13. The second part of verse 11 had convicted Beth, and she had mentally repeated it many times in the past week — "for I have learned, in whatsoever state I am, therewith to be content." Beth knew she must learn to be content with God's will for her life, but in all honesty, she also knew that she was anything but content. Dad had always been a source of strength for Beth, always willing to help her understand God's Word and to see its meaning for her life. She approached her dad at his desk in the living room. He was writing a letter to Michael, as he did every Saturday afternoon. Thoughts of Michael and how she missed his presence made her voice quiver a bit as she asked, "Dad? Can I talk to you?"

Dad looked up quickly at Beth, loving concern on his face as he noticed her tear-filled eyes. "Of course you can, sweetheart," he gently answered. "How can I help my favorite daughter?" Beth gave him a weak smile as she recognized the phrase Dad often used to cheer her up. He had used it the first time when Beth was only four years old. She had innocently asked, "Am I really your favorite daughter, Daddy?" "Of course!" he had answered. "Even if you are my only one!" The phrase had become a long-standing joke between them, but Beth was too miserable to get much comfort from it today.

"Dad," began Beth, "do you think maybe we could move again? If not back to Tennessee, maybe to some other place? A bigger town?" Those questions were not what Beth had intended to ask at all, but as she blurted them out, she realized that those really were the questions that filled her heart. Having asked them made Beth feel guilty. Especially when she looked at Dad and saw deep disappointment in his eyes.

Hurriedly she continued, "I mean, couldn't God want you

to go somewhere else now? We've been here a year, and the church is really well established. Someone else could take over here, and keep it going." Beth dropped her eyes and felt them fill with tears again. Why did she always cry when she talked about something important like this? It was frustrating that she was unable to control her emotions and express her thoughts in a calm and logical manner.

Dad was silent for a moment. Then he leaned back in his chair and quietly said, "God called us here, Beth. When and if He calls me somewhere else, I'll gladly go. But until and unless that happens, this is His will for us. I thought you had accepted that, and you were happier here now."

" I am. Or I was. But I'm missing Michael again, and friends, and, well, everything." She paused, then continued, "Besides, I'm getting older, Dad." Dad smiled at that, and Beth's face turned red. "Okay, not really old, but I will be eighteen in January. What do I do now with my life? We had always planned on courtship. Where do I find someone to court me? There's nobody here! I do want to get married someday — and well, I just don't see any hope."

"I see." Dad looked thoughtfully at Beth, then asked, "Do you believe that God can do anything, Beth?"

"Yes, of course. He is all powerful," Beth replied.

"Do you really believe that He can do <u>anything</u>, though, Beth? Do you believe that He can bring a husband to you without your help or advice?" Dad persisted.

Beth looked down. "Yes, sir. I know He doesn't need my help. I do trust Him. But I'll still have to meet someone, somehow. How can that happen if we stay here?"

"Beth, let me tell you a long story. Let's sit on the couch. This is going to take awhile, but I think it will help you." After Dad and Beth sat down, he reached over and patted her hand in a loving way. "Beth, I'm going to tell you two stories, actually. You are somewhat familiar with both of them. One is from my own life, and it involves someone else you know really well." As Beth gave her father a questioning look, he smiled.

"As you know, I was serving on the mission field as a young man. At thirty-four years old, everyone figured that I was a confirmed bachelor. I had an older couple working with me, who had never been able to have children, and they looked on me as a son. I not only had a great deal of respect for them, but also loved them dearly."

"This older couple, the Thatchers, had a niece who was a missionary at an orphanage in Belem, about 150 miles from our station. She had been a missionary for several years, but had only been in Belem for about a year. The Thatchers were anxious for a visit from her, as it had been many years since they had last seen her. Letters were fairly frequent between them, and the Thatchers had a deep attachment to Betty. Yes, the same Betty you know so well.

"When Betty finally came to visit the Thatchers, I spent quite a bit of time with the three of them. I had not been interested in being married, and had not expressed a desire to marry to these dear friends. So I was quite surprised to find myself thinking of your mother so much after she had gone back to Belem. And thinking of marriage very seriously. I prayed a lot about the idea, and after a few months, God led me to write to her — just a friendly letter, to see what kind of a response I would receive. She wrote back, and I thought I could almost hear her voice in the words on the paper. Memories from those two weeks she had been with us flooded over me. I really missed her. Me! The bachelor!" Dad laughed.

"I approached the Thatchers and asked for their help." Dad paused and laughed again. "I was sure they would be surprised, but they weren't at all! God gave discerning eyes and wisdom to that dear couple. They gladly served as spiritual parents to both of us, since both our parents were in the States. They helped us arrange a courtship, most of which had to take place by mail. And you know the happy ending to that story," Dad concluded.

"Yes Dad, but wasn't that a miracle? I know God could do the same for me, but will He? I think it would take a miracle for me to find a husband in Kanesville, and I'm not sure it will happen. I guess I'm scared it won't!" Beth twisted a soggy Kleenex in her hands that she had used earlier in an effort to stop her tears.

"Beth, there are a couple of things we need to correct here. First is the idea that you are going to find a husband. You aren't. If God wants you to get married, He will find one for you," Dad reminded her. "I won't find a husband for you, Mom won't, and you won't. God will."

"I know, Dad. I didn't really mean I would try to find a husband," Beth reassured him.

"I'm sure you don't think you meant that, Beth, but our words sometimes reveal what we really do think. Perhaps that is your trouble! You say you trust God to bring a husband, and yet you can't see how it will work out in these circumstances, so you are afraid. Is that trust?"

Beth was quiet. After waiting a moment, Dad began to speak again. "I said I was going to tell you two stories. The second one is about another young man who was of the age to marry. There were no young women living anywhere near him who were appropriate candidates for a wife. What was he to do? How could he find someone to marry? This young man's father trusted God completely, and God sent an angel ahead to prepare the way. The young woman that this young man married was provided by God at the right time. Circumstances would have suggested no way for this young man and young woman to meet, but God can do anything."

Dad reached over to his desk and handed Beth his Bible.

"Read Genesis 24, Beth. The entire chapter. The story of Isaac and Rebekah can still be a model for us today. When God wants you to marry, if He wants you to marry, He will bring a husband to you. There are many Christian families who are seeking the Lord's will in this area. It is my heart's desire that God will send a young man and his father to me, when the time is right. Then if you are willing, as Rebekah was, your courtship will take place. Let's begin now, Beth, to pray that God will bring your 'Isaac' at the time He has appointed. Let's ask Him to help you trust Him, and to wait patiently as He sends an angel to prepare the way. Can you do that, Beth? Can you wait for your Isaac?"

Beth's answer was found in her shining eyes.

Chapter Eight

*J*ust before supper that night, Mom found Beth in her brothers' room, helping them with a jigsaw puzzle. Mom beckoned to her. " Beth, I need you for a few minutes." Beth quickly followed Mom into the hall. "Come on down to the kitchen and I'll explain," Mom said with a smile.

Once in the kitchen, Mom lowered her voice. "I want you to walk over to Pearson's Corner Market for me. I thought I'd make peanut brittle for a treat after supper, but I don't have enough corn syrup."

"Peanut brittle!" Beth exclaimed. "I'll be glad to go, Mom. It's been a long time since we had peanut brittle. It would taste so good on a cold evening like this one."

"I thought so, too," agreed her mother. As Beth came up from the basement with her coat, she held a pair of boots in her hand.

"I can't believe all the ice still on the sidewalks from that freezing rain yesterday. I hope winter isn't here to stay yet."

"Oh, I don't think so, dear," replied her mother. "This cold snap is just a bit early. You be careful walking, though. You don't want to drop the corn syrup. And put your hood on. That wind is bitterly cold."

"Okay, Mom," answered Beth as she finished buttoning her coat. "See ya!"

Beth walked briskly out the door and into the cold air. The north wind felt like ice water being poured over her face when she turned the corner onto State Street. Head down against the wind, she hastened the length of the block, then paused before crossing the street. Beth glanced quickly to the left and right, eyes squinted against the sharp wind. Then stepping off the sidewalk, she took a few hurried steps before she slipped on a small patch of ice near the curb. Beth fell on her side, her right leg bent and her left leg extending into the eastbound lane of the street. Suddenly she heard a scream of brakes, and terrified, felt tremendous pressure on her left leg. Then for a short while, she knew nothing at all.

Cold and hard. Those were the first sensations that came to Beth as she regained consciousness. Something cold and unyielding was pressing against the right side of her face, and her cheek burned, as though fire was held against it. She made an attempt to lift her head from the cold hardness, but tremendous pain in her leg prevented her. Beth gasped, then cried out, and a man's voice gently said, "Don't try to move, little lady. Everything will be okay. You're all right. Just lie still. The ambulance will be here soon."

Beth opened her eyes and saw smooth black pavement. Several pairs of boots and shoes were close by, and one pair of knees, encased in blue jeans. The voice seemed to be coming from whoever was wearing the jeans. At first the voice sounded far away, but it seemed clearer to Beth as she tried again to raise her head.

"Don't move. Please don't move. You'll be okay. It will only be another minute." Someone laid their coat over Beth. "Listen — I can hear the siren now. Your leg is hurt. Just be really still, okay little lady?"

Beth whispered, "Okay," and then began to cry. Her tears were prompted as much by fear as by actual pain. Earlier today she might have told Dad she was getting older, but right now Beth wanted her mom more than anything else.

The siren was loud now, so loud that it hurt Beth's ears. Flashing lights cut through the gathering darkness, and more voices were overhead. "What happened? Is she conscious?" From the conversation around her, Beth had already learned that a car had swerved to miss her just as she slipped and fell. She must not have really looked carefully before crossing in the twilight, and her eyes had been squinted against the wind. The driver was an older lady, whose shaky voice repeatedly asked, "Will the child be all right? Is she all right?" Beth asked the blue-jeaned knees to tell the elderly stranger that she was all right.

Now a pair of knees encased in brown pants was kneeling beside the blue-jeaned pair. "Hello!" a cheerful voice greeted her. "My name's Tony, and I'm a paramedic. My buddy Dave and I are going to take really good care of you, so don't you worry. What's your name? Are you in a lot of pain?"

"Yes! Most of the pain is in my leg. It hurts so badly." After another brief moment of intense pain she continued, "My name is Beth Grant. My face feels like it's on fire, and I can't lift my head without terrible pain in my leg," Beth finished shakily. Her tears had stopped, and she tried her best to remain calmer.

"I know it's hard to believe, but in this case, pain is a good sign. Now just lie really still and don't try to move. Let us do all the work, in case your back is hurt, okay?"

After a few minutes of carefully checking her out, he added, "Beth, it looks like it's just your leg, but we don't want to take any chances. We're going to stabilize your fracture and keep you totally flat. To do that, we're going to install a cervical collar and strap you onto a back board. It's just precautionary. Then we'll strap the board to the stretcher. Okay?"

"Yes, sir," Beth replied. Then trying to blink back tears, she asked, "Can you call my mom and dad? Right away, please?"

"Sure, we're going to do that," Tony reassured her. "We want to get you out of the street first, then we'll get their name and call. Just relax, now. Here we go."

Beth was carefully lifted inside the ambulance and covered with a warm blanket. It felt so good to be cared for, even by strangers. Her leg was in terrible pain, as was the right side of her face, but Beth felt much better than she had a few minutes ago. Dave had taken her parents' name and address, and a few minutes later, reassured her that a dispatcher had already called her parents. Beth knew they would go straight to the hospital to meet her.

During the drive, Tony took her blood pressure and respiration every few minutes and started her on oxygen. He also continued assessing her condition and talked with the hospital emergency physician. "Can I have something for pain?" Beth asked meekly.

"We really don't want to give you any medication if we can help it, Beth. If you should need surgery right away, it might complicate matters. We'll be there real soon. Okay?"

She tried not to think about her leg, but instead to concentrate on answering the questions Tony asked as they drove along the now dark roads. Between questions, one phrase went through Beth's mind again and again - "for I have learned, in whatsoever state I am, therewith to be content."

"We're here, Beth!" Tony said as he hooked her oxygen into a portable tank. "That didn't take us long, did it?"

Beth wasn't sure how to answer that question. In many ways it seemed like it had taken forever to get to the hospital. With each bump in the road, Beth had felt tremendous pain from the jolt. Once, she had cried out but had tried not to complain much. She had been transported only about thirty minutes to a hospital in a nearby town of 30,000 people. She was about to answer Tony's question with a positive statement about how fast it had been and how much he had helped her, but was interrupted by Dave's conversation.

"Okay, Tony, we're ready. Release the lock and slide her

. . . really slowly!"

Beth felt pain again as the stretcher was slowly pushed to the back of the ambulance where Dave and several other men and women were standing. The icy wind rushed against Beth's face. *Why can't they have a nice emergency room entrance, like we had in Tennessee?* Beth thought to herself. *The hospital in Tennessee had a completely enclosed area for ambulances to drive into that was heated in the winter and air conditioned in the summer. Here, they only have a porch for the ambulance to drive under.* Beth felt the resentment and anger building inside her once again.

"Hello, Beth, I'm Dr. Pierce, the emergency room physician. We're going to take good care of you." Beth couldn't help smiling at Dr. Pierce. He was wearing a light-blue smock and had all kinds of instruments hanging off his clothes, and stuffed in his pockets. *I wonder if he knows what he's doing?* Beth thought to herself.

It wasn't long before Beth got her answer. Dr. Pierce was a skilled emergency room doctor and was able to diagnose Beth's problems quickly and efficiently. He directed his staff in a professional and caring manner and had Beth cleaned up, x-rayed, and changed into a gown with a minimum of pain on Beth's part. Beth was starting to feel foolish over her initial impression of Dr. Pierce and this hospital. They might not have been a large medical facility, but they did know what they were doing.

Dr. Pierce walked back into the examining room with a smile on his face. "Well, Beth, I see you're still here. That's good! I never like it when my patients walk out on me without saying goodbye."

Beth smiled at Dr. Pierce, even though her pain was coming back. He had such a kind and reassuring bedside manner. She felt she could trust him completely. "Yes, sir, I'm still here. What is going to happen to me, Dr. Pierce?

Are my parents here yet? Is my leg going to be okay? Why is my face hurting so much?"

Dr. Pierce smiled. "You sure know the right questions to ask, Beth! Let me give you some answers. First, your parents have been called and are on their way. They should be here any minute now. Second, is your leg going to be okay? I really think so, although we have to take a good look when the x-rays come back. You have several fractures that we will have to deal with, that's for sure. I do believe you will be able to walk again, though."

Beth cringed. She had no idea the accident had been so bad. "You mean that you aren't sure I can walk again?" she cried out.

Dr. Pierce had a calm, smooth voice. "There is no way to know yet, Beth. Let's neither of us jump to conclusions until we know for sure. Okay? I have seen people with much more serious injuries walk again. But we'll just have to see. Now, you also asked about your face. It hurts because you fell on the road and it's scratched up pretty badly. Nothing seems broken or dislocated in your face, though."

"At least that's good." Beth tried to sound encouraged, but it was hard for her. "What happens next?"

Before the doctor could answer, Mom and Dad came rushing into the examining room and to Beth's side. Beth involuntarily started to cry again. Mom cried also, and said, "Praise God that you're okay, honey. We've been praying so hard on the way here."

Dad was calm, but Beth noticed a few tears drop from the corners of his eyes. "How do you feel, sweetheart?"

Beth couldn't answer. She was so overjoyed to see her mom and dad that she couldn't speak. Dad gently stroked her hair. Mom continued to cry softly.

After a minute, Beth answered, "I'm okay, Dad. My leg hurts anytime it is moved and my face hurts pretty badly."

Beth suddenly felt exhausted and closed her eyes.

Dr. Pierce moved closer to the bed. "I'm Dr. Pierce, and I have been taking care of Beth. She's going to be okay. We have taken x-rays and they should be ready any minute now. Why don't you two just stay here with Beth and I'll be right back?"

"Yes, we will. Thanks." Dad pulled a chair over to Beth's bed and had Mom sit down. Dad continued standing and took Beth's hand in his own. Quietly and fervently he prayed.

In a few minutes, Dr. Pierce walked back into the room. "I have examined the x-rays and would like a specialist's opinion of them. There are several fractures, and we want to proceed cautiously so as not to do more harm. I've called Dr. Johnson, our orthopedic surgeon, to come in and examine the x-rays and Beth. He should be here in about thirty minutes."

While they waited for Dr. Johnson, Mom and Dad continued to pray. Beth opened her eyes to find them praying. She felt safe and loved, and drifted back off into an unsettled sleep. After a few more minutes, Beth felt another spasm of pain and cried out. Dad asked quickly, "Are you okay, Beth? Do you need something?"

Beth tried to ease the tension that she knew her parents must be feeling, and said, "I guess I just need to watch where I'm walking next time."

Dad tried to smile at that, but was still concerned about Beth's condition. Beth continued. "I'm sorry I wasn't more careful. I sure wish you didn't have to see me like this, and get so worried about me!"

"Nonsense," Mom said. "Beth, we're glad to be here with you. And it doesn't matter what you look like or what you've done. We love you, no matter what."

"Do you know when I am going to feel better, Dad? Has the doctor told you anything at all? Please don't hide anything from me."

"No, Beth," Dad quickly replied. "He hasn't told us anything at all. We're still waiting for Dr. Johnson to arrive and give us his opinion. I promise not to hide anything from you."

"Thanks," Beth said. "I sure don't seem to be doing anything right in my life, do I? You have to put up with a complaining daughter who wishes she was back in Tennessee. You have to listen to my fears about a future husband. I'm sorry I'm so much trouble."

Being a pastor, Dad had often stood by a patient's bedside and heard patients tell their parents or spouses that they were sorry for the trouble they had caused them. Again, he tried to reassure her. "You're not too much trouble, sweetheart. You know you're not. We all have accidents in life. They happen so quickly. I trust you're going to be okay. We must all trust in God." Then with a sparkle in his eyes, he added, "You might as well not feel sorry for me. Someday I am going to be sick or be involved in an accident. Then you can help take care of me. Okay?"

"Sure, Dad," Beth whispered, as the door opened.

In walked a man, who looked to be in his early thirties. "This is Dr. Johnson," Dr. Pierce announced. "He and I have been carefully studying Beth's x-rays."

"Hello, Beth," Dr. Johnson said. He didn't seem as friendly as Dr. Pierce, but his voice and mannerism suggested that Dr. Johnson had a great deal of confidence in himself. "I'm sorry about your accident. You must be Beth's parents?"

"Yes," Dad replied quietly.

"Well, good. I'm glad you're all here together," Dr. Johnson continued. "It appears that Beth has a displaced fracture of the proximal tibia and fibula with involvement of the peroneal nerve." At the confused looks of Beth's parents, he translated, "What that means is a break of the two bones in the lower leg just below the knee, and it has impacted a nerve that goes to the foot. Normally, I reset fractures myself. However, we don't have the latest technological equipment here that would allow me the precision I need for her specific case. I could reset them, but given the nature of the fractures, there is a chance that I might destroy some delicate nerves. To avoid that as even a possibility, I am recommending that Beth be transferred to the Mayo Clinic in Rochester. I could send her to Des Moines, but since we live this close to the Mayo, I would rather send her there. I've already called them and Dr. Jewett, one of the leading orthopedic surgeons in the country, is available to do the surgery as soon as Beth arrives. Also, due to Beth's condition, I think it would be wise to transport her by helicopter. If you agree, then we can order the helicopter right away. We need to get Beth on the way to recovery as soon as possible."

The news came so fast that it took a moment for it to sink in. Finally, Dad said, "If that is what you recommend, I guess that is what we should do. Right, Betty?"

"Yes, dear." Tears welled up in Mom's eyes. "Can I come along in the helicopter with Beth?"

"I'm sorry, Mrs. Grant, but our policies don't allow it," Dr. Johnson responded. "You and your husband would need to get to Rochester either by driving there or taking a commercial airline. I give you my word that Beth will be taken care of and given the best medical treatment possible."

Beth was confused. Why did she have to fly somewhere else? Why couldn't they just take care of her here? "Can't you do it?" she asked Dr. Johnson.

"Yes, Beth, I could do it. But I couldn't guarantee the outcome. At Rochester, we can increase our odds that you will be able to walk again. Isn't that worth it?"

Beth became frightened. "But why can't Mom come

along? She's not going to bother anything or anyone, will you Mom?"

Before Mom could answer, Dr. Pierce spoke up. "Beth, the rules are there for several reasons. First, there isn't a whole lot of room on the helicopter because of all the medical equipment on board. Second, the nursing staff that will accompany you needs to be able to focus all of its energy and attention on you. Any passengers that come along might interfere with that treatment by asking questions or trying to give advice. Third, our insurance does not permit anyone to be on board except the patient. You understand, don't you Beth?"

Dr. Pierce's kindness and gentleness worked wonders. Beth agreed and both doctors left the room. Mom and Dad started talking about how they could get to Rochester quickly. Beth was finally given a small dose of pain medication.

In about forty minutes, a helicopter was heard landing on the heliport outside the hospital. Beth had been moved to another room and was surrounded by doctors and nurses making final adjustments. Soon a young man entered her room, and said, "So this must be our patient. Hello, Beth. I'm Clyde, and I'm going to be your pilot for this trip. I've done this lots of times so there's nothing for you to worry about." Then quickly turning to the medical staff, he asked, "Are we ready?"

"Yes, everything has been done," Dr. Pierce replied.

"Okay, let's go!" Clyde said.

Before they rolled Beth's stretcher out the door leading to the helicopter, however, Dad said, "Can we have a quick prayer?" Then without waiting for an answer, he bowed his head. "Dear Father, thank you for loving us. Thank you that you promised never to leave us nor forsake us. Please help each of us to remember that promise in the next several hours. We leave Beth in your hands, Father, and know that you can accomplish all of Your holy will. Please give the pilots, doctors, and nurses wisdom. Bring us back together again safely very soon, dear Father. We give you all the glory, honor and praise. We ask all of these things in Your dear Son's name and pray that Your will be done over all things. Amen."

After Dad finished, no one moved for a minute. It was perfectly quiet except for the sound of the helicopter's rotors turning outside. "Thanks," Clyde said. "Let's go, crew!" Beth was loaded on the helicopter, and after a minute it lifted into the air and flew out of sight.

Dad hugged Mom and the two of them slowly walked back down the hospital corridor. "Watch over her, Father," he softly said.

Chapter Nine

"Ooohhhh . . . Ummmhhh . . . " Beth groaned and opened her eyes. She felt sick at her stomach and very disoriented. Where was she? Something sounded like a large fan blowing behind her but she didn't have the strength to turn around and see what it was. It sort of looked like sunrise to Beth with just a small amount of light entering her room. She turned her head to the right and saw rows of blurry little lights, some of them blinking off and on.

"She's waking up," a female voice said softly. "How far?"

"About another five minutes and we should be there," another voice answered.

Beth began to feel sicker and sicker. The room seemed to be swaying back and forth and each time it did, she felt worse. "What's going on?" she finally blurted out.

A kind-looking young woman in a blue jacket with "Life Line Transport" sewn on the shoulder moved into Beth's full view. "You're going to be okay, Beth. I'm Joan, and you're in a helicopter headed to the Mayo Clinic in Rochester, Minnesota. We are only a few minutes from landing and then we will help you out. I'm sorry the flight is a little bumpy tonight, but there's a lot of wind coming down from the northwest."

Beth could hear Clyde, the pilot, talking to the hospital landing crew about wind speeds, direction, and final preparations for landing. The talk was a little excited, probably due to the high winds they were experiencing. Joan noticed that Beth could hear the conversation and tried to divert her attention. "You'll feel better soon, Beth. We gave you a little more pain medication when the trip started because your leg hurt you so much. It's just wearing off and that sometimes makes patients sick."

Beth quickly returned to a state of full knowledge about what had happened and where she was going. "Why do things always have to go wrong for me?" she thought out loud. "We were just going to have some warm peanut brittle and now look at me!" After a second, she added in a bitter tone, "When am I ever going to enjoy life again?"

"I'm sorry you don't think your life is much fun," Joan said, as she turned to inspect the readings on several instruments at Beth's side. Apparently Joan had thought Beth was talking to her. "I'll bet things will look brighter tomorrow. You just have to learn to put more faith in yourself. Just keep telling yourself that things will look better and they will. I've seen it happen to me many times. The more you have a positive self-image the better you will feel. Your strength, your joy has to come from inside you." She stopped talking because Clyde was making his final approach to the helipad at the hospital. Joan sat down in a seat and buckled up.

That gave Beth a little time to think about what Joan had said. Did Beth's hope and faith really come from inside her? Could she change things in her life just by the way she felt about them?

'I can do all things through Christ which strengtheneth me.' Beth had learned this verse when she was only six or seven years old, and knew it to be true. The more she thought, the more she realized that Joan's words were not wisdom from Christ. Instead, Joan was sharing some New Age ideas. In spite of her pain and nausea, Beth's conscience was hard at work. She felt bad that she had not been a better witness for Christ in this situation. Instead, she had all but asked for worldly wisdom from this nurse.

Beth wanted to set the record straight and provide a

witness for Joan. She wished to tell her that a happy and joyous life was only possible through the help of God. However, as she was about to speak, the helicopter touched down. Suddenly, everything seemed to be happening at once. The helicopter's blades slowed and stopped while Clyde assisted Joan in stowing away medical instruments and positioning the oxygen line. The helicopter's door was opened, and Beth was carried though the cold, windy, dark November night into the hospital. She looked back for Joan, but never saw her again. Apparently, Joan stayed with the helicopter. Now Beth would never be able to provide a testimony of God's help and grace. Tears filled her eyes.

Her tears were seen by a tall thin man in a white coat. "You're going to be okay," he said. "Dr. Jewett's surgical team is standing by. Why, I'll bet they're the best in the world for this kind of injury! Yes ma'am, you couldn't be in better hands!"

Remembering her conversation with Joan, Beth suddenly exclaimed, "I'm in God's hands. I put my trust in Him." Pain caused Beth to stop for a second before continuing, "He can use this doctor to heal me."

The tall man didn't say anything. He, along with several other attendants, wheeled Beth's gurney down a series of hallways. As she was passing under one door, Beth noticed a sign which read: ABSOLUTELY NO ADMITTANCE! Surgical Teams Only Allowed Past This Point. "Please help me, Jesus," Beth prayed softly.

Soon Beth was in a bright, warm room. Oh, the warmth! It felt so good to Beth after being outside even for the brief time from the helicopter to the hospital doors. She realized that she was also probably cold as an aftereffect of the pain mediation she had been given on the helicopter ride. There seemed to be people everywhere in the surgery room. She tried to focus on what each person was doing, but finally gave up. Everyone seemed to have a specific set of jobs to do and they were doing it efficiently.

A rather short man finished giving the nurses some directions, then turned and spoke to Beth. "Hello. I'm Dr. Jewett. I've had a conversation with Dr. Johnson and I've also been studying the x-rays we received. We're going to be operating on you in a few minutes. This is Dr. Lindsey, the anesthesiologist for the surgery. These are Drs. Osborne and Rochelle, the orthopedic residents that are serving under me. They will be observing and assisting in this operation. What we will be doing is called open reduction and internal fixation — which means we will be aligning the bones, holding the alignment with screws and repairing the ruptured ligament. We'll be ready to start in about five minutes. Do you have any questions?"

For the first time in Beth's life, she couldn't think of a single question to ask. "No," she answered.

"Good," said Dr. Jewett. "Dr. Lindsey, I'll let you start getting her ready now."

Dr. Jewett turned and studied the x-rays more closely, carrying on a quiet conversation with his residents and pointing to various things on the film.

Beth became frightened. She felt so alone. *Why can't my parents be here with me?* she thought. Everyone seemed to be so preoccupied looking at their charts and instruments that she was tempted to shout out, "Hey, do you even remember that I'm here?" Suddenly, a Bible verse came to her: 'What time I am afraid I will trust in Thee.' Repeating this and remembering other verses from God's Word gave Beth a more peaceful feeling.

In a few minutes, Dr. Jewett looked around the room, then nodded to Dr. Lindsey. Beth turned to look at the large, round clock on the wall. It was 2:33. The middle of the night! How she wished she was in her own bed in Kanesville.

68

She tried to think of what her younger brothers might be doing now. *I wonder if they are asleep or* — Beth's thoughts came to an abrupt end as the anesthesia took effect.

Beth need not have worried about her brothers. They were safely asleep with Mrs. Newman watching over them. Her parents were en route to the Mayo Clinic on a hastily arranged charter flight. Several members of her church were awake, even at this late hour, praying that the God of grace and mercy might direct the surgeon's skilled hands.

Hours went by. Hours in which serious and potentially life-changing decisions had to be made about how to best mend Beth. Beth did not hear the surgeon's calls for instruments, or the periodic updates from Dr. Lindsey about her vital signs. She didn't hear the conversations between the surgeon and his residents or the constant beeps from the monitors. She didn't feel the instruments opening the area, adjusting her bones and repositioning the muscles and ligaments. She didn't feel the tight pull of the surgeon's needle and thread.

Thankfully, she didn't hear the surgeon's sad sigh as he turned and walked out the door. He had done all he could do. What more could anyone expect with such an injury?

Chapter Ten

$\mathcal{B}$eth reached for a glass of water. Before she could get it, however, her dad had it in his hands and was holding it so that Beth might drink. The water was cold and felt good going down her throat. An extremely dry throat was about the only aftereffect of the drugs used by the anesthesiologist. For that she was thankful. Beth had been told that many people experienced nausea, vomiting, and dizziness from the drugs.

It had been a day and a half since the surgery was completed. Beth had been in surgery for over four hours and then spent twelve hours in recovery. She honestly didn't remember a thing about any of that time now. The first thing she could remember was seeing her dad bring a bag of hamburgers into her hospital room about fourteen hours after the surgery was over. Apparently she had needed the many hours of sleep.

"Can I get you anything?" Dad asked.

"No, thanks Dad," Beth answered. "I just can't seem to get enough water." Then after a moment she added, "My cast feels too tight."

Thinking of her cast brought tears to Beth's eyes as she suddenly remembered the doctor's prognosis the day after the surgery. She had begged the doctor to be totally honest and tell her every possible long-term consequence of her injury. "You may be able to walk on the leg, but I can't promise it," he had said. "It will take months of intensive physical therapy and repositioning. I'm afraid it's going to be a long, hard road. It may be that you'll have to use a walker or cane. Also, some patients with nerve injuries like your's result in the patient being unable to hold the foot up well when walking, resulting in the toe catching on things. Sometimes, because of this muscle weakness, the foot tends to slap the floor when walking, creating an unusual gait. We'll just have to wait and see."

Beth looked at her cast again. She hated to complain, but her leg was in pain. She never dreamed she would be lying in a hospital bed with a leg that might never work properly again.

When the doctor arrived that evening, he looked exhausted. "Hello Beth," he said, trying to sound cheerful. "How is my patient?" Beth could see dark circles under his eyes and could almost hear his mind shouting, *I'm exhausted! Can't I rest?!*

"I'm doing okay, Dr. Jewett." Then, as he was looking at her chart, she asked, "Except that cast seems too tight. Do you think it could be?"

Dr. Jewett continued looking at her chart. He then studied her leg. After a minute, he said, "I'm sorry. It's not cutting off your circulation or anything vital. We want it to heal the best we can, don't we?"

"Yes sir," Beth answered, tears coming to her eyes. She was thinking again about what he had said after the surgery.

As the doctor left the room, Dad walked over to the bedside. "Beth, I'm sorry. But I know something that might make you feel a little better. I have to wait a while before I can tell you, though . . . "

Suddenly, the room's walls echoed with the shouts of two excited boys. "Hi, Beth!" John and Adam shouted together as they ran over to her bed. "We're here!"

"There's your surprise," said Dad.

Beth started crying softly. Tears of joy at seeing her brothers. How she loved them and had missed them. "Yes, I know you're here guys," Beth laughed and cried at the same time. "So does everyone else on this floor! Oh, how I've missed you."

After the initial exchanges the boys had exciting things to talk about. Things like the fact that their neighbor's water hose had frozen the night before, road conditions and the auto accident they had passed by, the health and status of their various pets, and what had come in the mail at home. Soon, however, the boys were engrossed in looking at Beth's cast and trying to figure out how her hospital bed worked. John summarized their feelings in one word: "Neat!"

"Yes, I guess you could call it neat, John," Beth answered sadly. "But it's not a lot of fun."

"I'm sorry you feel bad," John said, with tears suddenly starting to form in his eyes.

"Thanks, John," Beth replied. Then to change the subject she asked, "How did you enjoy your ride up here?"

Both boys talked about their trip to Rochester from Kanesville. They related again details of the accident involving a tractor trailer and a station wagon outside Albert Lea, Minnesota. Mr. Cooper had been so kind to drive them up. "He even let us have a milkshake for lunch!" Adam reported, then looked at Mom a little sheepishly.

"That's okay," laughed Mom. Adam looked relieved.

All too soon, the nurses came in and said it was time for Beth to get some rest. After having a time of family prayer and Bible reading, everyone left. Beth lay in her bed and reflected on the events of the past few days.

What did the future hold for her now? She had always wanted to be a wife and mother. Beth thought of her hope chest back home. Already it was filling with "treasures" for her hoped-for own home. Would anyone want to court her if she was crippled? Suppose she could never walk again? What if she spent the rest of her life in a wheelchair, or had to walk with a walker? Would there be a man who would want to spend his life taking care of her?

And children. Beth's eyes filled with hot tears. Would she

even be able to take care of her own children? Life looked so bleak. How could she hope to ever have a happy life? Suddenly she remembered Joan, the young nurse in the helicopter. "When am I ever going to enjoy life again?" That was the question Beth had spoken aloud in the helicopter, and it echoed in her mind over and over again. How she wished she could find Joan and give her a more positive witness for the power of Jesus Christ. Joan needed to know that New Age ideas could not provide peace and eternal life. "I just wish I could tell her about the power of Jesus," Beth whispered aloud.

"When God wants you to marry, if He wants you to marry, He will bring a husband to you." Dad's words of just a few afternoons ago floated back into Beth's conscience. The more she reflected on Dad's words, the more real they became. *I wanted to tell Joan of God's power. And it is God's power that can provide me with a husband, if it truly is His will. Dear God, please help me to trust fully in you for all things,* Beth prayed silently. *I'm so afraid! I want to tell others about You, but I can't be a good witness with fear in my heart. Help me not to be afraid for the future, through the power of the Holy Spirit. Amen.*

With a little more peace in her spirit, even though her leg was in pain, Beth drifted off to sleep.

Late the following afternoon, a quick brisk step was heard in the hall outside Beth's hospital room. Soon Dad stood beside her bed, smiling down at her. "Hello, favorite daughter! Mind spending a little time alone with your dad this evening?"

"Of course not! I'd love to. But where are Mom and the boys?" Beth questioned.

"Mr. Cooper took them out for an early supper. He's driving us home early tomorrow, you know, and I wanted to have some time alone with you before we leave."

"Yes, I know," Beth spoke quietly, trying to keep her voice under control. " It will be so hard to be here alone, Dad. You'll pray for me, won't you?"

"You know we will, Beth," Dad reassured her.

"Oh Dad, I'm sorry. I know you will. But without you all with me for the next few days, I'll be so lonely. Why did all this have to happen? Why do so many bad things happen to me?" Beth's eyes smarted with tears, and she turned her face away from her father, unable to meet his kind but unwavering gaze.

"So many bad things?" he repeated. "So many? I only know of one thing that has happened in your life that you could possibly call bad. The accident has been hard for all of us. You especially, of course. But as impossible as it may seem, try to remember that all things work together for <u>good</u> to those that love Him. Good, Beth. Not bad. God's Word is true, whether we believe it or not. And it is very important that you believe. You <u>must</u> trust Him now. This is a turning point in your life. Either you trust Him now, and move onward and upward on the Path with Him, or you may become spiritually crippled." Dad hesitated, then continued, his voice gentle but firm. "Spiritually crippled would be much worse than physically crippled, Beth."

"But Dad," Beth sobbed, reaching for his hand, "all my hopes, all my dreams . . . first we move, then Michael leaves, now this. What will become of me? What will I do? What if no one wants to marry me if I end up being crippled? I know God can do anything, but I'm so unhappy. I just want things back the way they were before, back in Tennessee. I was so happy then."

Dad was silent a long time. Thoughtfully he stroked Beth's hand, then gave it a reassuring squeeze. Sighing deeply, he looked at her with love in his eyes, and a determined look on his face. "Beth, you need to spend the next few days doing some very deep thinking and praying. You can't go on like this. You have made some real progress in the past two years, but it is time to take a big step forward. You aren't a little girl anymore. God's Word says that spiritual milk is for spiritual babes. It is time that you began to take in spiritual meat, Beth.

"You keep repeating a few words over and over. Have you really heard yourself? Do you really know what you are saying? I . . . I . . . me . . . me . . . my hopes, my dreams, I'm unhappy, what will I do, what will become of me. All your thoughts are focused on yourself. All of them. I suppose, considering the circumstances, that some of that is only natural. But you can't continue in that spiritual condition. You must ask the Lord to help you set yourself aside. Because that is what is in the way of your spiritual growth. Yourself. It always has been. It is for all of us. Jesus said that you must deny yourself, take up your cross, and follow Him. You are clinging to yourself and what you want, instead of denying yourself and clinging to what He wants. I know it is hard. It isn't easy for anyone. We are too weak to do it on our own. But remember that He has said that His strength is made perfect in weakness. Call on Him, ask Him to help you. He will answer. But you must truly want to set yourself aside. You must truly be willing to take His will for your own."

Dad smoothed her hair back from her forehead, something he had not done since she was a little girl. "What bad things have really happened in your life? Was God's gift to you of a loving home and Christian parents bad? Was His gift of brothers who love you and would do anything in their power to make you happy, bad? How about all the food and clothing He has always provided you? Or the warm houses He has sheltered you in? Are these the bad things that have happened to you? And above all that, He has granted you eternal life through the sacrifice of His only begotten Son. It is time you started calling God's gifts good. 'Every good and every perfect gift is from above, and cometh down from the Father of lights.' He has blessed you over and over again. You could have lost your leg. You could have lost your life. But He has spared your life. He has spared it for a reason."

"How can I find what the reason is, Dad? How can I know what He wants me to do?"questioned Beth, her voice calmer now, but still a bit shaky.

"He wants from you what He wants from all of us. Obedience and trust. If you will set yourself aside, and serve Him every day, in any way that He asks you, you will be doing what He wants you to do. When I said that He spared your life for a reason, I didn't mean that He spared your life for some unusual or exciting task, although that could certainly be true. But for most of us, it will be the task of simply glorifying Him in our daily lives. He tells us in I Samuel that to obey is better than sacrifice. And the way to find out what He wants you to do is to read His Word, carefully and with an open heart. Just thankfully accept from Him whatever He brings into your life. God gives good gifts to His children. And we have to trust Him that this accident is, somehow, a good gift."

"'Bye, Beth! See ya in a few days!" Adam waved as he walked out into the hall.

"Don't be too sad, okay? I promise to call you every night. Dad said we could," added John, lingering at the door.

"That will be nice, John." Beth swallowed hard, willing herself not to cry. She had spent much time in prayer after Dad left last night, and knew that to really set herself aside, she had to be as brave and cheerful as possible when she said goodbye to the family this morning. If she allowed herself tears, it would only make them feel worse about leaving her, and there was really no choice. Hotels were expensive, and it would be too long a stay for all of them. She was nearly eighteen now, which was certainly old enough to stay alone in a hospital, with all the medical staff there to care for her needs. Beth knew herself well enough to know that it would be hard for her not to give in to self-pity today, and make everyone feel sorry for her. Jesus alone could help her to pass the test of self-denial taking place right now. She was finding Him to be true to His Word — "I will never leave thee, nor forsake thee."

Dad and the boys stopped a few feet down the hall to say goodbye to the nurses, as Mom spoke her parting words to Beth. Mom smiled down at her, but her eyes were shiny with unshed tears. "Beth, I can always stay longer, you know. I know your dad will let me. I can sleep on the couch in the lounge right down the hall at night. I can be here all day to keep you company, if it's just too hard for you to be here alone."

The loving concern in Mom's face was a harder test than Beth had counted on this morning. She reached out and hugged Mom, breathing a silent prayer for the Lord to give her the strength to continue to deny herself. How she wanted her mother to stay! Yet there wasn't really anything she could do for Beth, except keep her company. Dad and the boys had needs also, and the dark circles under her mother's eyes told Beth that Mom really should go home and rest.

"Thanks, Mom. The Holy Spirit is with me, and angels are watching over me. I'm glad you can go on home with Dad. I think that's best. I'll see you soon. And I look forward to being home before long!" Beth added, smiling.

"I look forward to that too, darling. I love you. See you soon." And with a last quick hug, Mom was gone.

Chapter Eleven

$\mathcal{B}$eth certainly felt alone for the rest of the morning. Her family did not own a television, and Beth did not want to begin watching it now. Mom and Dad had found a couple of books and magazines at a Christian bookstore in town, but somehow Beth didn't feel like reading them. She did spend quite a bit of time reading her Bible and found that she drew comfort from reading many of the Psalms. During the next five days, Beth fell into a routine of sorts. Between the schedules of meals, doctor checkups, and regular nursing tasks, Beth wrote a long descriptive letter to Michael in Brazil. As she spent more time in the Word and in prayer, her phone conversations with those at home began to change in tone and content. She tried to take a real interest in subjects that her younger brothers enjoyed, and saved them small tokens from her room to make them laugh.

Finally, the day arrived for Beth to be discharged and sent home. Though it had been less than a week since she had seen her family, it seemed much longer. What a happy journey it was, with her parents and brothers surrounding her once again. Every effort was made to make Beth's trip home a comfortable one. Adam and John must have each asked her a dozen times, "Can I do anything for you?" Dad had made a special place for Beth in the back seat of the van, piled high with soft blankets and pillows to keep her leg elevated. In spite of the discomfort her leg caused, Beth's spirit joyfully sang, "I'm going home — going home!"

Later, at home in her own bed, Beth quickly became sleepy. The trip home had been more tiring than she had anticipated. Her spirit was still singing joyfully within her, however, as she drifted off to sleep. "Home. I'm home."

As the weeks passed, Beth spent much time on her bed or on the couch, resting her leg. She found that there were still many ways the Lord could use her, in spite of the fact that she was unable to move around easily. Indeed, some of the ways He used her seemed to be due to her relative immobility. She spent much time helping her mother homeschool the boys, as well as planning and organizing projects for the summer. Dad found her to be a big help in some extra correspondence that needed to be done. And Beth had time to write several articles for the girls' magazines that had encouraged her so much. Now, she felt, the Lord had given her the opportunity to be an encouragement to others.

With Michael she began a new relationship even though South America was many miles away. While they had become closer than ever during the past summer, she had still been the "taker" and he the giver. As she spent more time in the Word, her letters expressed her spiritual growth. Now that she had experienced real pain and disappointment, she found herself able to better understand some of the trials and loneliness he faced. Beth began praying faithfully for Michael each day, much deeper and more specific prayer than in times past.

In his many letters, Michael shared with her more about the lives of the individual boys he worked with, and she became a real prayer partner for him. Her dad's words came back often to her — "What bad things have really happened in your life?" Beth realized more each day that she had been tremendously blessed by God. The boys at the City of Youth had very sad and hard things in their past, yet many had given everything to God and now lived for Him. Could she do less?

Lamentations 3:22-23 became very real to her. It seemed to Beth that each morning she was able to see, through the eyes of her spirit, more mercies that God had granted her. Instead of focusing on the way her life was not fitting her plan, she began to ask God to reveal to her what

His plan was for her life each day.

Beth's leg gave her plenty of cause for spiritual growth. The cast was hot and uncomfortable on her leg, and itched almost unbearably. Two Bible passages helped Beth bear with the constant discomfort. Romans 5:3-5 was now taped onto the dresser beside her bed, and she saw it so often that it was not a hard task to memorize it.

And not only so, but we glory in tribulations also: knowing that tribulation worketh patience; And patience, experience; and experience, hope: And hope maketh not ashamed; because the love of God is shed abroad in our hearts by the Holy Ghost which is given unto us.

Beth felt that God was speaking to her every time she read that verse. She prayed that God would use this tribulation to work patience in her, so that she might be ready for any other situation that could come into her life in later years. The second passage was Philippians 3:13-14. She taped this one onto a lap tray used for writing letters.

Brethren, I count not myself to have apprehended: but this one thing I do, forgetting those things which are behind, and reaching forth unto those things which are before, I press toward the mark for the prize of the high calling of God in Christ Jesus.

Paul's words helped Beth to remember that she needed to focus on the prize before her, and that she should never allow herself to dwell on the past. The past was past. She could not go back to the days before the accident, and no amount of wishing could make it so. If God had willed that the accident should happen, then it was wrong for her to covet the past.

Every time Beth thought of the accident she couldn't help but remember her conversation with Joan, the helicopter nurse. Would it be possible to write her a letter? And what would she say if she did write?

Finally, Beth asked her father if there was some way to locate Joan's address. A few days later, Dad walked into the living room. "Here's the address you were looking for, sweetheart." He handed Beth a slip of paper.

"Thanks, Dad," Beth answered, then hesitantly she added, "Dad, if I draft a letter to her, do you think you could look it over and offer any suggestions?" Dad readily agreed.

In a few days, with help from Dad, the letter was ready.

Dear Joan,

You may not remember me, but I'm a patient with a leg injury you transported to the Mayo Clinic several months ago. I want to thank you for your efforts at making that ride as pleasant as possible. You tried your best to cheer up a pretty discouraged patient.

I'll never forget something you said, though: "Your strength, your joy has to come from inside you." I'm afraid I didn't take the time to share with you where my joy and strength actually come from. May I do it now, in this letter?

My source for all strength and joy comes from Jesus Christ, my Savior. To be honest with you, at one time, I would have given the same answer you did. But some years ago, through the work of the Holy Spirit, I realized that I didn't have the power I needed to live a life filled with joy. I knew that I was a sinner and deserved eternal death as punishment for my sins. I needed God's forgiveness. But how could I possibly be forgiven? Could I do good things to try and make up for all the bad things I had done?

No, I couldn't get forgiveness just by doing good things, no matter how hard I tried. I still couldn't live a perfect, sinless life. And I knew that a holy and perfect God would accept nothing less. What could I do? I could do nothing to deserve forgiveness, yet God showed me His loving grace by allowing His Son, Jesus Christ, to die for my sins.

"For God so loved the world, that he gave his only begotten Son, that whosoever believeth in him should not perish, but have everlasting life" (John 3:16). Jesus Christ was given to us by God the Father, as a sacrifice for our sins. God tells us in His Word, the Bible, what we must do to become acceptable before Him, and to be forgiven. "That if thou shalt confess with thy mouth the Lord Jesus, and shalt believe in thine heart that God hath raised him from the dead, thou shalt be saved" (Romans 10:9). "If we confess our sins, he is faithful and just to forgive us our sins, and to cleanse us from all unrighteousness" (I John 1:9).

Forgiveness is found only in Jesus' death for us, His life given for ours. I can't explain why He would do that for us. No one deserves it — that is why it is called grace — it was an undeserved act of mercy. Jesus died for me, and He died for you, also.

For many years now, Jesus has been the Lord of my life. That means I try my best, with His help, to do His holy will and obey God's commandments. And do you know what else has happened? He has given me strength to meet whatever comes my way. I also have joy. Joy cannot come from inside me because I will it to be there. True and lasting joy can only come from God Himself.

I hope all of this makes sense to you. I would be happy to write more if you write me back. I hope you, too, will find the strength and joy that can only come from accepting Jesus Christ as your Savior. I'll pray for you.

My leg may never be totally healed. In fact, I may never

82

be able to walk normally again. But I know that God is in control of the future and I trust Him. He has promised in His Word that He will work this situation for my ultimate good. To Him I give all honor and glory.

Beth

Beth stopped and prayed for Joan before she sealed the letter. *I'll probably never hear from her*, she thought. *But perhaps God will use this in some way to bring Joan to Himself.* Whatever the outcome, Beth felt a great peace in knowing that it was in God's hands, and that she had obeyed His prompting by writing to Joan.

Beth's cast was removed in time for her eighteenth birthday. What a relief it was to have it off her leg! And how strange her leg looked. Beth's eyes filled with unbidden tears as she viewed it for the first time. Her leg was scarred and slightly shrunken from lack of use. Even the skin looked strangely shriveled, somewhat as her fingertips did after a long hot bath. Beth asked Dr. Johnson about her leg after he had examined the x-rays in his office.

"Don't worry, Beth," he reassured her. "Your leg will regain most of its original appearance with time, although the scar will remain. The next step is to get you into physical therapy, so that we can get those muscles ready to walk easily again."

"Do you think I'll be able to walk just as well as I did before the accident?" questioned Beth hesitantly. She had to ask the question, although she was afraid of the answer.

"Well, Beth . . . " Dr. Johnson paused. "From looking at the x-ray, I'm not worried about your ability to walk. You shouldn't have much trouble at all, once you begin physical therapy." He stopped looking at an x-ray and looked directly at Beth. " I believe that you will be able to lead a normal life, and that your leg will not prevent you from any everyday activity. Your injury, however, was quite extensive, and you will likely be left with some stiffness and a limp. What degree of stiffness or limp is impossible to know right now. Only time will tell."

Before the accident, that statement would have devastated Beth Grant. But the Lord God Almighty, Maker of heaven and earth, had taught her much since then.

She returned the doctor's gaze, and he was amazed to see a smile on her face. "God has spared both my life and my leg, and I'll be able to walk again. I am so very thankful for that." Beth glanced down at her leg. Looking up into Dr. Johnson's eyes once more, she quietly added, "I will try to leave the limp in His hands, to do what He sees fit."

Months followed. Months in which Beth spent many hours working with a physical therapist, then repeating the exercises at home. Just to be able to walk about the house again filled her heart with joy. Discouragement did set in from time to time, however, as Beth remembered how easily she had always walked before. Progress sometimes seemed slow as day followed day. Beth learned to lean on the Lord, and found that His grace was sufficient indeed.

In late February, Michael wrote to tell his family that he felt God was leading him to stay at the City of Youth as a full-time missionary. While everyone was happy about this decision, they knew it would be hard not to have him home this summer. His next furlough wouldn't come for over a year. Yet, God was in control of all things.

Chapter Twelve

etty, you've got to read this!" Dad swiftly raced from the front porch to the kitchen. "You've got to read this!" he echoed.

Mom dried the dishwater from her hands. Beth continued to wipe dishes, smiling at Dad's bounding enthusiasm. "What are you smiling at, Robert?" Mom asked, quickly reaching for the letter in Dad's outstretched hand.

Dad didn't say anything as Mom glanced at the return address. "The Foreign Mission Board?" Even at this question, Dad refused to speak. Mom quickly pulled the letter from its envelope. She sat down at the old-fashioned kitchen table she loved so much and began to read.

"Why Robert, that's great!" Mom said, jumping up and hugging Dad. "You're going to be a busy man!"

"And a happy man!" Dad added quickly. "Just think. I'm responsible for the next two years."

Beth's curiosity got the best of her. "Can I ask what is in the letter?" she asked, looking from one parent to the other. "What did you say about two years?"

Mom happily handed the letter to Beth. The letter explained that Dad was going to serve as furlough coordinator for the Foreign Mission Board of his denomination for the next two years. "What will you do, Dad?" asked Beth. "Decide who gets to take a furlough and for how long? Or what?"

"No," Dad smiled. "That administrative stuff is handled by someone else. My job is to coordinate furloughed missionaries with speaking engagements across the country. I'll make sure they have free places to stay and people to share their experiences with. And," he added, grinning broadly, "I'll also make sure some of them get to taste the hospitality of Kanesville and our humble abode!"

"Did you know this was going to happen?" Beth asked.

"Well, I did let it be known that I would be glad to serve the Lord in this way, if that's what you mean," Dad replied. "But I didn't formally apply for the position or anything like that. About a month ago, I got a call from the Director of the Foreign Mission Board asking if I would, in fact, be willing to serve in this way. I knew they were probably considering other men also. I didn't mention anything to anyone because I didn't want to disappoint them. But now it's official!"

"Will you quit your church? Is it a paying job, Dad?" asked Beth. She was secretly afraid that the family would be uprooted again to a new location.

"No, I will keep my church, Beth. As far as pay goes, the job comes with a very small stipend that is mostly used to offset long distance phone bills and other expenses like that. A lot of the work will fall on my correspondence secretary," Dad concluded.

Beth didn't remember Dad having a correspondence secretary. In fact, he didn't even have a secretary. Before she could ask, however, Mom interjected: "Do they provide a correspondence secretary for you, or do you get to pick one?"

Dad took the letter and read it over again. "I was just seeing if the letter said anything about it, but I see it only mentions the fact that they will provide support for a part-time secretary at minimum wage. During the phone call I had, the Director said I would probably be able to choose my own secretary."

After a few more minutes, Dad left the kitchen to deliver the good news to his sons and friends. Mom and Beth finished doing the dishes, then worked on sewing for a while. As Beth sewed, a thought entered her head that just wouldn't go away. *No . . . it's silly even to ask,* she thought.

After supper, Mom and Dad sat and talked about what the new position would mean to their family. They discussed the use of Michael's bed for visiting missionaries to their area, and mentioned some friends they hoped to see in the next two years. Dad was having fun just thinking about what lay ahead.

"Say, Dad," Beth began, without much confidence, "you mentioned that you would need a correspondence secretary. What kinds of things will that person do?"

"Oh, I haven't even thought about that. Let's see. I suppose the secretary would help me with all the letter writing, phone calling, and filing. Lots of typing, I guess. Actually, I suppose it's time to start looking for someone to fill the slot. I don't know how long it might take to find the right person."

Beth went back to her knitting. This was a lot harder than she thought it was going to be. Why was it so hard to ask her dad? Mom and Dad continued talking about some missionary friends they knew.

"Dad, how old does the secretary have to be?" Beth asked.

"I don't know. I don't suppose it really matters to me. I'll just want someone who will be very conscientious about the job. Oh, and someone who has a real heart for missions. Otherwise, I don't suppose they would do a good job. You know how it is; if your heart is in something, you are usually much more careful about your work."

Beth continued knitting, but she purled a row where she should have knitted and had to unravel some of her work. Finally, with great meekness, which was uncharacteristic for Beth, she asked, "Dad, do you think that someone like, . . . that someone like, . . . like me might be able to do the job?"

Dad smiled at Mom. "I do believe that Beth is interested in the job of correspondence secretary. Don't you think so?"

"It sounds like she might have some interest in learning more about it," Mom replied cautiously.

"Yes, Dad," Beth admitted. "I am interested. But," she quickly added, "if you want to hire someone else or don't think I could do the job, I won't be hurt." With a red face, she turned back to her knitting. Her mind, however, was whirling. What would her dad say?

"Well, I would love to have you as my partner in this, Beth. I know a lot about your communication skills," he said laughing, " and think you could certainly handle the writing and calling. The filing part I could teach you. And isn't it great that you know how to type? Tell you what, let me talk to the Director tomorrow and see if it is a problem for me to hire my own daughter. Okay? I'll also need to talk this over with your mom. It sounds like a good possibility to me."

Beth was very excited. "Thanks!" In fact, she was so excited that she left the room after a few minutes to take a stroll around the block. Everything seemed so beautiful with spring finally here again. And now, here was a chance to do something very useful with her father. Life sure seemed to be looking up for Beth.

The next afternoon, Dad found Beth in the garden area, planning where she would like to plant things for the summer growing season. "Well, there's my correspondence secretary!" Dad exclaimed.

"Oh, Dad!" Beth's face lit up, and she moved slowly toward him. Her limp was not getting better, even with the warmer spring air. "Am I really?"

"Yes, you are. And when you're ready to start, I would like to go over some things with you."

"Before we start, Dad," Beth began, "Can I ask you something? I'd really like to donate my salary to Hope Unlimited. All of it, if that's okay with you and Mom."

At Dad's surprised and pleased expression, she continued, "I have everything I need. God provides all my needs through you. I . . . I have so much, and they have nothing." After a pause she continued, "How can I keep anything for myself when there are still homeless boys on the streets?"

Dad smiled at Beth. "I can tell that you are changing your diet, Beth."

With a puzzled look on her face, Beth echoed, "Diet? Did you say changing my diet?"

"Yes!" laughed her father. "From milk to meat. Remember?"

"Thank you, Dad," Beth smiled back at him. "I still have a long way to go. It helps to know that you are watching over me and praying for me."

"Every day that God grants me, Beth. Every day that He grants me." Dad gave Beth a hug. "Well! We have a family from Peru coming home in about a month and we need to finalize their arrangements. Are you ready? It may be a lot of work."

"I'm ready, Dad," Beth replied. The two of them walked into the house and began to discuss how they would work together.

During the next several weeks, Beth was kept busier than she had ever been. In addition to working with Dad, she still had to keep up with her sewing, gardening, and other house work. But no one could have been happier. Beth felt like she was doing exactly what the Lord had for her to do at this time of her life.

Dad scheduled the furloughs of the Ketons from the Philippines, the Glavors from Syria, and the Mixons from Kenya. Each schedule took an incredible amount of time and energy to put together. In addition to considering the requests of churches, he had to accommodate the wishes of the missionaries. All wanted most of their time to be based in the general vicinity of their hometowns in the U.S. To facilitate this, Dad had to communicate not only with churches but also with the missionaries a great deal. Beth found it great fun to write to such exotic sounding locations as Hamah in Syria, Baguio in the Philippines, and Losho in Kenya. The boys, of course, treasured the foreign stamps that arrived at the Grant house on a regular basis.

Before long, Beth felt more confidence in her role as correspondence secretary. She was no longer anxious before placing a long distance call, or typing an important letter. The deadlines no longer seemed so ominous and she learned to relax and enjoy her job more each day. Dad said more than once, "We make a pretty good team, Beth."

In June, Mr. and Mrs. Winston, missionaries serving in Kiev in the Ukraine, stayed at the Grant house. They had many wonderful stories to tell about how God was changing lives in the former Soviet Union. "The fields are white to harvest," Mr. Winston said several times during his visit. "There are so many people who want to learn about Christ that we can't meet them all. Also, we need more men to go and help disciple the new converts in the Christian faith. I'm afraid their communist upbringing makes many of our truths hard to grasp."

Of course, Dad's job was to get that kind of message out to the churches and the people. He eagerly helped churches set up weekend missions conferences, as well as finding time for the Winstons to share during regular church services. Of course, he also had to spend time leading his own congregation and working with the many other missionaries who were going to be on furlough. It was a busy month!

June was busy for Beth also. In addition to being Dad's correspondence secretary, she worked closely with Mom in cooking and hospitality for the Winstons while they were visiting. For anyone who has never taken care of the needs of another family it may not sound like a lot of work. But it surely is. There is more laundry to do, larger meals to plan and cook, more dishes to wash, and greater needs in cleaning the house. Beth loved it.

As the summer progressed, more missionaries visited with the Grants. Beth sometimes almost felt overwhelmed with the amount of responsibility she carried. The gardening took a lot of time, but her brothers were beginning to be a great help to her. As she looked back over the last few years, she realized that moving to Kanesville had many positive effects on her life. For one thing, it broke her dependence on her friends. She had learned to love to spend time with her family and serve them. Also, it had forced her to come to grips with obedience and following the will of her father (as well as her Heavenly Father), instead of selfishly following her own wishes and desires.

She also thought about the changes that her accident had caused. Beth could truly say now that she did depend on the Lord Jesus Christ for all things in her life. Her leg was not improving as much as the doctors had hoped. She was going to limp the rest of her life, and might even become crippled again later in life. But the mighty God of the universe knew her needs and would provide for her according to His holy will. No, she was no longer alone. The only time she had been alone was when she was trying to accomplish things in her own power — then she was truly alone and truly helpless.

Chapter Thirteen

"Honey, here's something neat," Dad exclaimed from his desk in the living room. Mom and Beth were doing some mending while the boys read. It was cold outside. Quite cold, even for late January, and the wind was howling. The Grants were glad to spend Beth's nineteenth birthday around the warmth of a fire.

"What's that?" Mom asked, holding several pins in her mouth.

"Do you remember Margaret and Randy Benton? They were missionaries to Durazno, Uruguay while we were in Brazil. They had four children."

"Sure, I remember them. Margaret and I wrote each other for years. She was such an encouragement to me about living for Christ and trusting in Him for everything. Then we both got so busy that our letters trailed off and finally stopped." Mom got excited. "Are they still missionaries? Are you going to be setting up their furlough?"

"I don't know if they're still missionaries or not," Dad replied. "The reason I mention it is that I have some paper work here for a Daniel Benton. He's been on the mission field for four years. Didn't they have a son named Danny?"

"Yes, I believe they did. They called him either Dan or Danny, I can't remember which. Where is Daniel serving?"

"He is a missionary in the Atacama Desert region of Chile. Let's see . . . if that's the same boy, he would be . . . how old now?"

Mom thought a minute. "Hmmm. As I remember it, their Dan was about five years older than Michael, so that would make him about twenty-six years old now. Do you really think that could be him?"

"I don't know," said Dad. "Daniel Benton is not a really unique sounding name, so I suppose it could be someone else. My correspondence secretary will find out for me. Right, Beth?"

"Sure, Dad. When I write him our first letter, I'll ask him. Do you want me to do that tonight?"

Dad rubbed his chin. "I suppose there is no hurry. Just whenever you get a chance, Beth."

Beth stood up and stretched her left leg. Then she walked over and hugged her dad. "Now is a good time, Dad. I know you'd like to find out. So would I. It would be exciting to work with someone you and Mom know."

About three weeks later Dad received a reply from Mr. Daniel Benton. He tore open the envelope quickly, causing John to stare at him. "What did you get, Dad? A free vacation to Hawaii?"

"Something better," answered Dad after reading for a few moments. "A letter from the son of a very good old friend." Then heading to the bedroom where Mom was cleaning, he read the rest of the letter.

Everyone was excited to learn about Daniel. The excitement was made more intense when Dad explained that Daniel wanted to have most of his furlough in the upper Midwest, close to many of his relatives and friends. That meant that the Grants might get a chance to see him, and perhaps even have him stay in their house.

"Where are his parents?" Beth asked. "Are they still missionaries to Uruguay?"

"Daniel explained in his letter that they are retired now, but still spend a lot of energy speaking at missions conferences and going on short-term mission projects to South America. Daniel was their youngest child, and they are a few years older than we are. They live in a suburb of Chicago, Illinois. "

"Wouldn't it be nice to see them again?" thought Mom out loud.

As the correspondence continued, Daniel's itinerary was firmed up. He would spend most of his time in the Chicago area, but would take a few trips to other areas to speak at missions conferences and retreats. Dad was able to schedule a week-long missions conference in a larger church about 35 miles from Kanesville. Although several families in that church volunteered to house Daniel, he decided to spend the evenings at the Grant home in order to get reacquainted with his parents' old friends.

It was a cold weekend in mid-March. The weather forecasters were calling for possible snow, with blizzards not being ruled out. Travelers were cautioned to stay tuned for later warnings and watches. The Grants were concerned. Would Daniel be able to get to their house before the storm hit? Would the weather have an adverse impact on the missions conference? God was in control of the weather as He was in control of all things. He was able to accomplish all of His holy will.

On Saturday afternoon, the snow starting blowing in from the northwest. At first it was just a few flakes. Before long, however, the flakes were much bigger and the sky started to become almost totally white. Dad walked from window to window, checking to be sure that everything outside was all battened down for the storm. As he was looking toward the street, a car drove cautiously down the road. It came to a complete stop at the house next door. The driver seemed to be having trouble seeing. Finally, the car moved ahead a little and stopped in front of the Grants' home. Since the snow was already piling up on the passenger side of the car, the driver had to roll down the passenger side window in order to see the house number clearly. He then rolled up the window and pulled into the Grants' driveway.

"That must be Daniel," Dad said, as he moved toward the front door. "Hey everyone, I think Daniel is here!"

The rest of the family gathered at the window while Dad went to the car and shook the driver's hand. Soon, the two men were in the hallway, brushing snow from their clothes.

"I would like you all to meet Daniel Benton. This is my wife, Betty."

"Hello, Mrs. Grant. I certainly remember my mom talking about you many times."

"This is my daughter, Beth, and these are two of my sons, John and Adam."

"It is a pleasure to meet you," said Daniel. Then turning to Dad he continued, "I was afraid I wasn't going to make it here before the storm really hit. We are almost in white-out conditions right now. My, it feels good to be safe in a warm, cozy house on a day like this." Then he quickly added, "I hope my staying here won't put you out much."

"We are thrilled that you are here!" Dad exclaimed with obvious sincerity. "Daniel, you are welcome at our house anytime, for as long as you care to stay." Then he stated, "But what are we doing, making you stand in the hallway. Come in! John, take his coat and hang it up, please. Beth, why don't you make Daniel a hot cup of coffee? I'll just jump out there and bring in his luggage."

But Daniel wouldn't hear of Dad carrying his luggage, and quickly went to retrieve his single suitcase and garment bag. "Now I can take my coat off and get comfortable," he smiled.

Daniel, Mom, and Dad sat in the living room, talking about Mr. and Mrs. Benton. Mom expressed her desire to see them again. "Well, that may be possible," Daniel said. "I know they would love to see you again. They had no idea you had moved up here to the Midwest. The last they knew you were living in Tennessee. What brought you up here?"

Dad related the story of their move and his home mission activity. Daniel listened with great interest. It was obvious that Daniel truly had a heart for God and the spreading of His kingdom. He asked Dad a number of questions about his ministry and the trials and victories he had experienced.

At supper, Daniel related some of the things he had been able to do in Chile with the help of God. Dad listened closely. It seemed he could never tire of hearing someone relate a missionary adventure. Once, as Daniel was describing a faith-stretching episode, Dad winked at Mom, indicating that he really liked this Daniel Benton.

That evening, a phone call came with the decision that, due to the weather, the missions conference wouldn't begin until Monday evening. While Daniel was disappointed, he still expressed happiness that he could spend more time with the Grants.

On Sunday, the Grants worshiped at home, as did many other Christians in town. The storm had left most roads totally impassable. Although crews were out working, it would take many hours to get the streets safe enough for travel. Dad led his family and Daniel in worship of the risen Christ. It was a special time for everyone.

The rest of Sunday was spent in many conversations with Daniel. Daniel seemed totally relaxed in the Grants' house, even leaning on the counter while the boys were washing dishes. He grabbed a towel and said, when he was told he didn't need to help, "Listen, I want to help. I enjoy pitching in where I can. It makes me feel useful. Back home, in Chile, I do quite a few dishes, I can tell you!"

That evening Daniel participated in family devotions with the Grants. As family members prayed, they asked God to bless Daniel's week-long missions conference. John echoed the feeling of everyone when he prayed aloud, ". . . and thank

you that Daniel can visit with us and that he is so neat . . ."
Daniel truly was a "neat" man of God.

The missions conference went well the next week. Daniel was well respected by members of the congregation and several again asked him to stay at their house. However, Daniel always replied, "Thanks so much. But I prefer to just stay with the Grants on this trip."

When the week ended and it was time for Daniel to head back to Chicago, all of the Grants were a little sad. Dad spoke for the family when he said, "Daniel, we feel like we've all made a strong new friend in Christ. You're welcome here anytime you can come. We love you and will pray for you often. May God richly bless you."

Daniel expressed a similar love for the Grant family. Then he stated, "I hope I can stop back by before I return to Chile. Maybe I can even come back with my parents. We'll just have to see. As you know," he said, looking at Dad with a smile on his face, "I have a pretty busy schedule of churches and conferences to visit. But I'll see what I can do. You are always welcome to see us in Chicago, too."

After Daniel drove away, John asked, "Hey, Dad? Can we go to Chicago and see Daniel? That would be lots of fun."

Dad looked thoughtfully out of the window before answering. "I wish we could, John. But I don't see any way of doing it just now. My work for the Foreign Mission Board is pretty much going to tie me down to home for the next year and a half. Remember, I told you all about that when I took the position."

"Yes sir, I remember. I was just hoping we could see Daniel again, Dad."

"Well, so do I, son," Dad replied. "It's in the Lord's hands, John. We'll just have to wait and see."

Chapter Fourteen

"Dad! Wait, Dad!" John ran out of the house waving his arms over his head, trying to attract his father's attention. Robert Grant rolled down the car window, smiling at his youngest son. "What is it, John? What do you need?" John almost shouted in his excitement. "It's Daniel! Daniel Benton! He's on the telephone right now, and he wants to talk to you. Hurry, Dad! Maybe he's going to come and see us again!"

"I'm sorry to disappoint you son, but you'll have to ask him for a number where I can reach him later, and I'll call him back. The Olsens are waiting for us to come to the hospital, to help get Mrs. Olsen home and settled again. You know that Mr. Olsen needs me, because those steps up to their door are still rather slick this afternoon. Explain to Daniel the situation, and I'm sure he'll understand. Tell him I'll try to call around seven this evening, if that's convenient for him."

"And John," Mom added, leaning over Dad's shoulder, "It's really cold out here, even if it is April. That wind is really strong. If you and Adam go out, please put on a coat."

"Sure, Mom. We will. And Dad, don't worry, I'll be sure to remember to repeat the number back to him." John grinned, and Dad grinned back. Last week John had answered the phone when another missionary had left a message for Dad to call him back. Dad was surprised to hear a voice at the other end of the line greet him with, "North Toledo McDonalds! How can I help you?" The mystery didn't take long to clear up with a check of the area code map, but it seemed destined to become a longstanding joke in the Grant family.

Later that evening, Dad called Daniel Benton back at the

number John had taken, and was pleased to recognize a familiar voice on the phone. "Randy! Is that really you? It's been many years since I heard your voice, but I don't think I could ever forget it."

"Robert! How good to hear from you. Daniel couldn't tell us enough about you and Betty and the wonderful time he had with your family a few weeks ago." Randy Benton and Dad talked for a few more minutes, then Randy exclaimed, "But here I am spending your money, and Daniel is the one you called to speak with. He's standing here beside me, just waiting to get his hands on the phone."

Dad laughed. "I would sure love to spend some time talking to you, too, though. It would be great to reminisce together, wouldn't it?"

"It sure would. As a matter of fact, we were thinking ... well, here, let me give the phone to Daniel and let him tell you about his idea." Randy Benton relinquished the receiver to his son, and Daniel had to laugh at the reluctant look on his father's face.

"Mr. Grant? . . . Thanks for calling me back. As you might remember, I have a speaking engagement in Des Moines on Sunday the 24th. My parents were thinking of accompanying me on that trip, and since it is just a few hours south of you, we thought we would check to see if we could impose on your hospitality. They would really enjoy seeing you again, and so would I."

"Why, Daniel, this is wonderful! Of course you can all come. This will be such a treat for us. I can hardly wait to tell Betty. And I must tell you that John will be walking on air all week! You surely did make an impression on that young man! When can we expect you?" Dad made a quick note of when the Bentons hoped to arrive, then hung up the phone and went to find his family. He knew the excitement his announcement would bring, and it gave him great pleasure to make it.

At his end of the line, Daniel hung up the phone and turned to his parents with an even greater degree of pleasure on his face. "It's pretty obvious that he must have said we were welcome, son!" Randy Benton laughed. "But remember, this is all in the Lord's hands. All of it."

"Yes, I know Dad," Daniel answered. "But it still may be the first step."

The 22nd of April was the warmest day Kanesville had enjoyed for many months. The doors and windows were open, allowing fresh spring air to sweep through the house. Beth and her mother felt suddenly energetic as they prepared for the Bentons' visit, and everything was in readiness long before lunch.

Early afternoon found the Grant family gathered on the front porch, enjoying the sunshine. Suddenly Daniel's car pulled around the corner, and Robert Grant was on his feet immediately. "They're here! Here they are, Betty!" he called through the front door to Mom, who had stepped inside to answer the phone. Soon everyone was talking and introducing. The years that had gone by seemed to almost vanish in those first minutes, as the Bentons and Grants renewed their old friendship. Something very special hovered around the group, and Beth truly felt that it was the presence of the Holy Spirit. She liked the older Bentons right away. In fact, they reminded her somewhat of her own parents. She knew that the conversations this weekend would be filled with interesting stories of missionary life. How she looked forward to them! It was hard to remember the time in her life, just a few years ago, when those kinds of conversations would have held no interest for her.

That night, Beth made her family's favorite meal, lasagna. After everyone was finished, Daniel grabbed a stack of dirty plates and challenged Adam and John. "Bet you can't keep up with me on drying and putting away while I wash."

"I'm not sure that's really fair. The boys haven't had lots of practice — although I certainly think it's about time they did! Maybe I should help them," suggested Beth.

"We can do it! Of course we can! You just sit and watch. Let's go, Daniel!" urged Adam. Soon the boys and Daniel were laughing and making the suds fly. In what seemed to be an amazingly short amount of time, the kitchen was clean. Even more amazingly, all the dishes were still intact!

Saturday morning found Beth up early. She had grown accustomed to very early rising when there was company at the Grant home, and received a great deal of pleasure from providing hot and inviting breakfasts for their guests. Moving quietly, she began preparations in the kitchen, but she leaned over too far once to get a pan out of a low corner cupboard, and her weak knee gave her some pain. Wincing, she rubbed her knee, and the pan she had started to dislodge suddenly slid out of the cupboard and onto the floor, taking several others with it. *I bet that will wake them up!* Beth thought ruefully. Listening intently, she could hear nothing above her, so she gave a sigh of relief and continued to work.

An hour and a half later, everyone had gathered around the table. After the blessing, the group sat enjoying breakfast in the soft sunshine that was already making its presence known in the fragrant kitchen. "By the way, Adam," remarked Daniel with a serious look on his face, "what do you use to catch those big noisy mice that live in your house?" Adam started laughing, but looked completely mystified. Mom, however, looked horrified.

"Mice? Did you say mice, Daniel?" Looking at Dad, she exclaimed, "Honey, do we have mice? I thought we were finished with mice in the house when we left the mission field." Mom gave an involuntary shudder, and looked helplessly at Dad.

" I'm not sure, but I think that Daniel was referring to a BIG mouse, dear. A really big mouse. A mouse that is up early fixing breakfast when we have company," grinned Dad.

Beth began laughing. "I'm the mouse, Daniel. I tried to be quiet, but, well, I guess the phrase "quiet as a mouse" doesn't refer to me. I'm sorry if I woke you. Of course, if you would rather not eat muffins that have been handled by mice . . . "

Daniel winked at his dad, then replied, "Oh, I guess I can make an exception. It would be a shame to miss these applesauce muffins, especially since they are the best I've ever eaten. I'll try to overlook any paw prints." Everyone laughed.

A few minutes later, Daniel had a chance to hold a quick conversation alone in the hall with his father. "She's got a sense of humor, Dad. It didn't bother her at all. This family is really special. I'm not trying to influence your opinion, though," he finished.

Mr. Benton laughed. "Not much! You're right, though. She doesn't take offense easily. Did you ever stop to think what you would have said if she had? What if you had hurt her feelings?"

"Wow. I really didn't think of that. That is a blind spot I have," replied Daniel. "I suppose I didn't worry about it, because the week I spent here told me quite a bit about all of them. I certainly don't know everything, though. Anyway," he continued, "she seems to have a sense of humor and doesn't let herself be overly concerned with everyday mishaps. That would be a big advantage in a different culture."

Randy Benton had only time to smile and nod his head before John came out of the living room. "There you are! Dad wants to know if you would all like to ride over to the state park for the morning. It's only about fifteen minutes away, and we could walk some of the nature trails." John's voice was enthusiastic, and Daniel smiled at him, then answered for both of the Benton men.

"That sounds great. I'll run up and get a jacket and be right down. Can I get something for you and Mom while I'm up there?" he added, looking at his father.

"Thanks, son. I'll go find your mother and see if I can hurry the women along. Might be a pretty big job, though, if they are talking while they work. Come on and help me, John," Mr. Benton finished.

That evening the two families enjoyed a time of prayer and the reading of God's Word together. Daniel thanked God silently for allowing him to learn more about the Grant family, and asked the Lord for continued guidance in the decision ahead. His parents had the same unspoken prayer in their hearts, unknown to the others kneeling there. And so, God was honored and His blessing sought in a matter that was yet to be revealed to those around them.

Tuesday evening, Beth thoughtfully swished her hands around in the dishwater as she searched for any stray silverware that she might have missed. Why was she allowing herself to dwell on the Benton family so much today? They had been gone since early Sunday morning, and more visitors were expected this weekend. A young couple who were missionaries to Taiwan were coming on Saturday, and Beth felt that she needed to be able to concentrate on the preparations for this new company. Every time she had a rather routine task, however, that allowed her mind to wander, wander it would.

That day at the park had been just lovely, Beth reflected, warm for late April, and the nature trails had not even been muddy. Both families had felt quite comfortable and at ease together. Then when the Bentons had left early Sunday morning for Des Moines, a real sadness had descended on Beth's spirit. She could not seem to shake her feelings of loneliness, in spite of the many lectures she kept giving herself. Beth sighed. Maybe after the dishes were finished, she could find some game to play with the boys, or a book to read, or a dessert to make.

As she headed upstairs to find her brothers, the phone rang. Beth knew that Dad was in the living room and would answer it. Continuing up the steps, she heard him greet whoever it was, but didn't hear the name. *Must be that couple who will be here on Saturday*, Beth decided. *They said they would call about midweek to let us know when they would get here.*

"Robert? Randy Benton. Have you got a few minutes to discuss something?"

"Why, sure I do, Randy. I always have time for you. But to what do I owe the unexpected pleasure of your call?" Dad asked curiously.

Daniel's voice was now heard on the other end of the line. "Well, sir, we sure do hope that you'll think this call is a pleasure! We, uh, that is I . . . well, when we came last weekend, we came to see all of you, of course, but we also came with a special purpose in mind. Mom and Dad wanted to see you again, and wanted to meet all of your children. Especially Beth. I had told them all about your family, and how much I thought of everyone, and I needed them to pray with me about something. I had been praying for the past few weeks . . . this is harder than I thought it would be! Dad, don't you think it's time for you to take over here?"

"Yes, son, I think it is! Robert, Daniel has been waiting and praying for a wife for several years. As you know, our family has always been committed to courtship, and I know that you have the same commitment for your family. When

Daniel led the mission conference a few weeks ago, he didn't come with the intention of looking for a wife. As he spent the week with you, however, he felt that God had led him there so that he could meet Beth. After he came back here, he spent much time in prayer for a couple of weeks, then confided his hopes to Margaret and me. We accompanied Daniel on his trip to Des Moines so that we could renew our friendship with you, and at the same time meet and observe Beth. We prayed about the matter quite a bit before we came, and have continued to pray for the past few days. All of us believe that God is continuing to lead Daniel to court Beth, but of course, His will has not been fully revealed to us yet. We would like to ask you and Betty to pray, think about the possibility, and talk it over. Then if you are in agreement with us, let Beth know and ask her if she is willing."

There was silence at the Grant end of the line for a few moments. Robert Grant's voice was rather shaky as he replied. "Randy, this comes as a pretty big surprise to me. A good surprise, but a surprise nonetheless. Please don't get me wrong! I think the world of Daniel, and I am honored at your request. As a matter of fact, I have to admit that Betty and I have already had some conversations about this very thing. I guess I wasn't thinking that things would happen quite so fast."

"I understand, Mr. Grant," Daniel broke in. "And I don't want you to think that I would try to rush things. I am willing to wait until you are sure that it is the right time, if you do decide that I may be the right husband for Beth. I hope that the answers from God, you and Mrs. Grant, and Beth are all "yes" to our courtship, but I know that you may not be willing to give her up anytime soon. I had hoped that maybe while I am in the States, we would have plenty of chances to see each other, and that it would work well for our families to spend more time together. But you just take your time. We'll wait and pray."

"Yes, Robert," added Mr. Benton. "You can rest assured that we will pray. Not that your answer will be 'yes', but that God will give you wisdom and discernment. We truly want God's will to be done in this, and not our own."

"Thanks, Randy. I know that. I know I can trust you. Which already begins to point the way to the answer, doesn't it? I'll get back to you. I'll get back to you just as soon as we believe that we know what God would have us do." Robert Grant's voice sounded stronger. " And thanks for calling. Why don't we pray together right now over the phone, before we hang up? Heavenly Father, You know our hearts, and You know us better than we know ourselves. Give us wisdom in this situation, and help us to do Your Will, and not our own. Thank you for bringing the Bentons back into our lives, and allowing us to know Daniel. Please bless him and grant him patience as he waits for an answer. And help us all, as we are helpless without You. In Jesus' Name, Amen."

Upon Beth's return to the living room a little while later, she was surprised to find her parents on their knees next to the couch, obviously praying together in low tones. Beth immediately turned around and went back to her room. What could be going on? *I hope Mrs. Olsen is all right*, she thought. *Maybe that was what the phone call was about. But surely Dad would have gone over if they needed him. What could it be?* Realizing that the Lord knew the concern on her parents' hearts, she knelt by her bed and asked Him to have His will in whatever was happening. She then asked Him to make her a comfort and help to her parents in any way possible, and to keep her from asking them any questions unless they chose to confide in her.

Chapter Fifteen

"Beth, could you come into the living room for a few minutes when you finish up?" Dad questioned, as he looked in on his daughter. Beth turned from the last pot she was scrubbing at the kitchen sink.

"I'll be glad to. I'm just about through here. Be right with you," she smiled. Hanging the pot back on its hook against the brick chimney, Beth looked around the room to make sure she had remembered to sweep. Satisfied that the job had been done "as unto the Lord," she turned out the light and joined her parents in the next room.

"Come on in, sweetheart. Have a seat. Mom and I need to talk to you about something important." Dad cleared his throat, and hesitated a moment. "Beth, you have really matured so much in the last few years. Especially since your accident, although you had begun to make good progress even before that. You have become a beautiful reflection of the love of Christ. Your mother and I have been praying for many years that the Lord would mold you into a godly woman, and we are thankful to see that He has done just that."

Dad was quiet for a moment, then he continued. "He has opened the eyes of others to see the same traits in you that we have observed. I told you a couple of years ago that neither you nor I would find a husband for you, but that it would be God Himself. Mom and I are very glad that the Lord has opened the eyes of one young man in particular. That young man is hoping that you will one day join him as his helpmeet. You promised that you would wait for God's choice, and you have been very faithful to that promise. God will reward you for that. Mom and I have prayed about this for several days, and we believe that He is leading toward the possibility of a courtship with Daniel Benton," Dad finished.

Beth sat in silence, her eyes wide. "Daniel!" She seemed to be unable to get out another word for a moment.

"Yes, Daniel!" Dad repeated, smiling broadly. "He and his father telephoned on Tuesday evening. They have been praying about this for several weeks, and Daniel has asked permission to court you."

"Daniel! Oh, Dad!" Her eyes filled with tears. "It seems too good to be true. God is so good! Oh, He is so good to me!" Her face full of happiness, and eyes lit with joy, she turned to her mother. "Mom!" Beth grabbed Mom and hugged her. "Mom, isn't it wonderful? I just can't believe it! Daniel is the most wonderful person I have ever met. How could he want me? What an honor!"

Mom's eyes were also filled with joy, in spite of the tears that flowed from them. She hugged Beth, but could not speak a word. Looking helplessly at Dad, she finally managed a weak laugh. "I know, I know. Women and tears of happiness. It doesn't make sense. But I can't help it."

"That's okay, honey," Dad comforted. "I expected it! And if the truth were told, I pretty much feel the same way myself. I guess I don't have to ask Beth if she is willing to be courted by the aforesaid Mr. Benton. I believe her words have already given her away! You'll need some time to pray about it, though."

"Yes, sir. I will, I promise." Beth's face was very pink, and she lowered her eyes. "The truth is, Dad, that I have already prayed quite a bit about it. But not as though he were going to court me. I have been asking the Lord to help me not think about Daniel, or the possibility of courtship with him. I have been telling the Lord that I want to continue to wait for His choice, and that I know Daniel might not be the one He has for me."

Shyly she looked up at Dad, with a glow of excitement on

her face. "I know it wasn't wise of me to even let the possibility enter my head. But I am human! On the other hand, could it be that God allowed some of those thoughts because He knew all along that Daniel would ask to court me?"

Dad smiled. " I don't really know how to answer that one, Beth. Of course, it is possible that He allowed it. I would think that He might have, simply because you have been so faithful in guarding your heart and thoughts. Try to remember, however, that we still aren't sure of His will in this. All of us — the Bentons, Daniel, your mother and I, as well as you, believe that the Lord is leading you together. If we didn't feel fairly sure of that, we would not pursue this courtship. It isn't just a different kind of dating. But until you and Daniel have actually courted, and all of us have discussed many things together, we can't know God's will. Let's pray together right now, before this goes any farther."

Together Beth and her parents knelt, seeking the Lord and His blessing and direction. After they had all prayed, they sat down once again. Beth had a sudden thought. "Dad, when the phone rang a couple of evenings ago, was that the call from Daniel? I came down the steps and saw you and Mom praying, and so I went right back upstairs." She paused for a moment. "I'm sorry. I shouldn't even ask. I wasn't trying to pry or anything."

Mom nodded her head. "It's okay, Beth. Yes, that was the phone call. We were pretty surprised, just as you were. But after much prayer and many conversations, we feel that God is leading in this. Now it's your turn to pray."

"Yes," added Dad. "No matter how you feel right now, I want you to give this serious prayer. Let us know when you feel sure. We'll call Daniel whenever you are ready."

The next few days were busy ones for Beth. Dave and Kim Jackson arrived early on Saturday morning, and stayed until Monday. There were meals to help with, and conversations to enjoy, but Beth made sure that she left the group early enough each evening to spend time alone in prayer. She felt a real peace as she prayed, and the Lord brought to her mind many of the character traits listed in the Bible of those who belonged to Him. Daniel seemed to possess them. He was truly an answer to her many longings. God's choices were best. How she thanked Him for His good gifts to her.

On Tuesday morning, after the family had finished breakfast, Beth asked them all to stay seated for a few minutes. "What's up?" questioned Adam. "You've had a huge smile on your face all morning, like you have some big secret. Are you going to tell us what it is now?"

"Yes," laughed Beth. "I'm going to tell you what it is now." Turning to her father, she looked into his smiling face. "I suppose you already know what I'm going to say, though! I'd like for you to place a long-distance phone call to Daniel Benton. Right now, please."

"I'll be glad to! Do you plan on telling the boys first, or just letting them listen and be surprised?"

"Let's just let them listen and find out," Beth decided, with a wink at Mom. "I have a feeling they will be listening pretty closely to any conversation you have with young Mr. Benton. Isn't that right?" she asked John.

"I think Daniel Benton is the neatest guy I ever met," John replied seriously. "But what is going on? Why is Dad supposed to call him?"

"Just listen quietly, please. If you are able to stay quiet that is." Dad grinned at the boys as he dialed.

Chapter Sixteen

*L*ook at the size of that building, Adam! Wouldn't you hate to be a window washer on a windy day up there?" John craned his neck, trying to see the top of the skyscraper from the car window.

"I bet there aren't many guys who'll do it. This is supposed to be the Windy City, you know. I think they'd have to pay me about a million dollars an hour, if it was my job. Why do the Bentons want to live in such a big city, Dad?" questioned Adam, also trying to see the top of the Sears Tower.

"The Bentons don't actually live in downtown Chicago, Adam. We're just taking you through here to let you see what the city looks like. You can tell your children someday all about it. Unless, of course, you decide to take that million-dollar an hour job washing windows," Dad laughed. "In that case, I suppose they would be able to see for themselves. They could wave to you from the sidewalk while you sway in the wind up there!"

"Now don't go giving them any ideas!" exclaimed Mom. "That's just the sort of thing that appeals to boys. Next thing you know, they'll be wanting to find out the job qualifications, so they can start training. I can just see them now, rigging up some sort of rope and pulley contraption, and hanging off our roof to practice."

"Hey, that does sound like fun!" enthused Adam. "Maybe we ought to try it when we get back home."

"See what I mean?" laughed Mom. "Forget it, Adam. I'm too old to stand the strain!"

The Grant family was on its way to the Benton home,

located in a suburb of Chicago. They had been invited to spend a few days there, to further the friendship between the two families, as well as to allow more time for "courtship conversations," as Dad called them. Daniel would be there all week, before spending a week in Kansas City, and Dad felt that the Grants could spare several days away from home. Beth was looking forward to being a guest in the Benton home, not only because she enjoyed those who lived there, but also because of something Mom had told her.

"Margaret Benton has a special gift for hospitality," Mom had said yesterday. "I've never been quite able to put my finger on it, but there is just a special feeling at her house. I've never visited her in the States, but in South America we stayed with them twice, for a few days each time. Even though most people in this culture would have considered their dwelling to have been quite humble, I felt . . . well, I felt as though I had come home after a long time away. Almost like those old-fashioned pictures — where a soldier is walking up the sidewalk to a cozy looking house with a front porch, and maybe a wreath on the door. Do you know the kind that I mean? Just looking at the picture somehow tells you that there is a mother there who loves her boy, and that he has dreamed of home for months." Mom suddenly sounded choked up, and stopped talking. She had turned back to the stove, where she was stirring a pot of stew, and Beth knew that in Mom's mind, Michael was that son in uniform. True, he was engaged in a different type of war, but he was indeed a soldier. It brought to Beth's mind the verse, 'Thou therefore endure hardness, as a good soldier of Jesus Christ.'

Beth hoped to observe Mrs. Benton closely, and learn what she did to give people that kind of a welcome. Mom had always been a good hostess herself, so if she thought Mrs. Benton had a gift for hospitality, it must be a very special one indeed. If the Lord did cause Daniel to become her husband, she would need all the help and instruction she could get from godly older women. Just thinking about the possibility of becoming a missionary's wife gave Beth a few butterflies. Then the Lord brought Daniel himself to her mind, and she felt reassured. She wouldn't be alone. God would be with her, and she knew from experience the truth 'I will never leave thee nor forsake thee.' Not only would the Lord be with her, but He would provide a husband for her that was a godly man, a strong spiritual leader. Daniel was cheerful, kind, dependable, and truly loved God and His Word.

A little later, Dad pulled into the Benton driveway. The Benton house was small and old-fashioned looking, with well-kept flower beds and large trees surrounding it. A white picket fence enclosed the small back yard, and from the sidewalk Beth could see a clothesline, filled with white sheets billowing in the breeze. Daniel leaned over the gate that led to the back yard. "Hello!" he greeted the Grants. "We're all back here on the patio, enjoying the sunshine. Come right this way. We'll get your luggage later, right guys?" he finished, grinning at the boys.

"Right!" smiled eleven-year-old John. "We saw the Sears Tower and everything. It was fun, but I sure am glad that you don't live downtown. This is so much nicer."

"I think so, too," replied Daniel. "Of course, I don't really live here, you know. I am just staying with my parents this year while I'm on furlough." By this time the group had joined the elder Bentons on the patio. "It's very different from my little house in Chile. But both of them are nice, because both of them are God's provision of shelter for His children."

"I think the boys would probably enjoy seeing the pictures you have of your house, Daniel, and the beautiful mountains around it," suggested Mr. Benton.

"That's a good idea. Why don't you all sit down and eat up the cookies Mom has for you, while I go inside to find them?" Daniel smiled at them as he went in the back door, with a cheerful wink at Beth. Beth felt the butterflies start again. She was sure that God was leading in this, but it felt a bit awkward just now. Nobody had said anything about the courtship, although there was really nothing in particular to say. Dad had already called Daniel with Beth's decision, and everyone had expressed their happiness. *What did you think they would say?* Beth asked herself. *Welcome to the first official courtship weekend?*

After the cookies had been eaten — although devoured was more the word for what John and Adam had done to them — Beth felt more relaxed. She realized that everyone else had been at ease from the moment they had arrived.

Daniel's pictures were very interesting, but Beth just looked at them as she would any other pictures. Until she suddenly remembered that she would be living there if she and Daniel married. She examined more closely each one of them, and those pictures immediately appeared quite differently to her eyes. *Is that what I would be living in? It looks so plain and bare.* Her eyes turned to look again at the pretty flower beds, the green grass, and the Bentons' white cottage. Disappointment crept over her face as it crept over her heart.

Daniel noticed the change in her countenance, and remembered that the Grants had left the mission field when Beth was only eight. He wondered, not for the first time, how she would adjust to a different culture and way of life. He believed that she would give herself fully to God in this matter, but surely there was some way he could help her. Perhaps his mother, as well as her own, would be able to help her most. They would understand better how a young woman might feel. Some girlhood dreams might be hard to leave behind, even for someone as dedicated to the Lord as Beth seemed to be.

Later that evening, Daniel excused himself from the

group in the living room. Old photo albums were being opened, containing pictures of the Benton family on the mission field. Both mothers were in the kitchen, making popcorn and talking about their plans for summer gardens.

"I need some help," Daniel began when they paused for a moment. "I have a subject that sure needs to be brought up in some way, but I'm not certain how to go about it. Beth seemed awfully disappointed when she saw the pictures of the house in Chile. I guess I should have expected that, and prepared her before I showed them to her. But perhaps the disappointment would have been there, anyway. Did either of you have a hard time adjusting to missionary housing, and leaving the culture here? What do you suggest?"

"That's been many years ago!" his mom said. "But I guess I probably did. Your father and I had been married for five years before we went to Uruguay. Perhaps it was easier for me because I had already had a chance to have a home here." Mrs. Benton smiled at her son. "Although that might have been more of a disadvantage. I had to leave quite a few things behind, and learn a new way of housekeeping."

"My situation is a little different from your mom's. I had never had a home as a married woman in the States. I went as a single woman to South America, and married there, after several years as a missionary. So I suppose that I was already somewhat used to the living conditions." Mrs. Grant looked thoughtfully toward the living room. "You know, maybe we can bring this up when we come in with the popcorn. It's really best to address it now if possible, before Beth's mind has a chance to dwell on it very much."

When the three of them rejoined the group, Mrs. Benton picked up one of the albums. "Oh, this brings back memories of our first place!" she exclaimed. "Randy, do you recall how hard it was to rig up a clothesline for me? There seemed to be no place for one that either wasn't in the way, or didn't invite

115

all the native women to comment on my skills as a laundress. Living on the mission field certainly was different from living in the States. It took a little while to adjust." Mrs. Benton paused, then added with much emotion, "But the rewards were well worth the effort."

"I remember," chuckled her husband. "You had a lot of things to get used to. Like concrete walls that never seemed to stay in one piece. They always had cracks running along the seams. Remember how Terry used to say he could see if it was raining outside just by looking through the cracks?" He took a bite of popcorn, then continued, "And it took you a long time just to do the wash, besides making meals or bathing small children in the washtub. We had to heat water for everything in those first few years, and I was busy, too, so you didn't have much help."

"The Lord was my helper. I found out that I could do without a lot of things that I had thought were bare necessities. I was called to be your helpmeet, to help you in whatever the Lord called you to do. His grace is sufficient. I soon learned that many of the adjustments I had were with my own heart. I had to believe that God knew what was best for me, and if He did not provide something, I did not need it. That was hard to learn, but things were much easier once I accepted that. 'But my God shall supply all your need according to his riches in glory by Christ Jesus.'" Mrs. Benton smiled at her husband. "Some things are much easier here, but I still miss the feeling of making a real difference in the day-to-day lives of those people."

Daniel nodded. "I think I know what you mean, Mom. But the Lord is using you here, to make a difference in the daily lives of people who live here. These people are just as important as those. I do understand how you feel, though. There are so few Christians in the countryside of Chile. I feel a real responsibility to be there. And I feel it is a real privilege, too." Turning to Beth, he continued. "I know you would have a real adjustment to make, just like Mom did. But the same God who was her Helper is yours, too."

Beth did not answer for a moment. She so wanted to make everyone think that she would not even have any difficulty at all, but that wasn't honest. She had to be honest. If she wasn't open with Daniel and the Bentons now, it would be due to pride on her part — an inability to admit that she was less than perfect. Looking at Mrs. Benton, she asked, "Did you think you would have trouble adjusting before you went to the mission field? Did it take you by surprise, when you saw the house that you would be living in for the first time?"

"I think it did surprise me. I'm afraid that it's rather hard to remember now, but I had not seen many pictures of things before we went, and the ones I did see, I probably saw through rose-colored glasses. Just the thought of being a missionary's wife, helping people in a strange country and culture, appealed to me greatly. I didn't really stop to think about what life would be like there. Oh, in a general way I did. I had to buy supplies, and I was told what to expect. But I just didn't really let it sink in too much until I was actually there. Just trying to keep up with all the work and changes in lifestyle kept me very busy. I was probably too tired at first to think about it very often." She laughed, and everyone laughed with her. "Perhaps the best way to prepare yourself is to learn to work hard, and give thanks while doing it. And not to pay a lot of attention to outward appearances of your surroundings."

Mom joined the discussion now. "You know, it's probably not wise for women to daydream — I think that is a weakness we all have. I know I have often done just that, and then been disappointed when things didn't live up to my imagination. I really think that is part of bringing into captivity every thought to the obedience of Christ. It is difficult to be ready to obey Him if we already have planned out what we would like. I hope I'm not discouraging you, dear," she finished sympathetically.

Beth shook her head: "No, not at all. Isn't that funny? I was afraid to admit that the pictures look, well, sort of barren and depressing to me, but now that I have, I already feel better. Maybe the Lord is showing me how childish I am, to hang onto ideas of what I have always wanted. After all, houses on this earth are so temporary. We have a home that is waiting for us in eternity. And by going to these people, perhaps some of them will also have a home waiting for them there."

Daniel's face was wreathed in smiles. *Thank you, Father*, he prayed silently. *Thank You for helping her. How good You are to help us all. Continue to help us during these next few days to draw closer to you and to find other things that we need to discuss.*

There were many other topics that needed discussing. The conversations became much more relaxed, however, after that first evening. Beth asked the Lord to help her be open and honest in every subject that arose. She was able to ask Daniel many questions about his life in Chile.

"What about the food there? Will I need to do a lot of gardening?" Beth asked. How glad she was that she had at least a few years of experience behind her in growing food. *And I never dreamed that I would be on the mission field myself in just a few short years*, Beth thought, as she recalled how Mom had told her about growing much of their food in Brazil.

Daniel, too, was thankful that Beth had learned quite a bit about gardening. "Yes, we do have to grow much of our food there. I'm located about three hours from Antofagasta, and the truck isn't always dependable. I usually go in once a month, but often I am taking someone with me — or several someones! So there isn't always a lot of room for supplies."

Beth found that she would also have to learn a different way of cooking. The meals would be much less varied, with a heavy emphasis on corn, beans, bread, and potatoes. Later one evening, after she had gone to bed, Beth wondered what it would be like to marry someone who had a regular job in the States. She could cook the meals she liked best, and live in a house she enjoyed. Then thoughts of Daniel came again to her mind. She very much trusted him, enjoyed his company, and believed that she would be happy being his helpmeet. Should she let such things as choices in food and surroundings affect her decision? How trivial they really were in the light of eternity!

Beth silently thanked God again for the many events in her life over the past three years. Michael leaving for South America, the move to Iowa, the accident, the giving up of old dreams of her future life — all these things led back to her father's favorite theme, the Lordship of Christ. "Beth, make it your goal to have Jesus pre-eminent in every part of life," Dad had often told her. "If He is truly Lord of your life, He is Lord of every part — we are to reserve nothing to ourselves." Lying quietly in the darkness, Beth saw that Jesus had taught her many lessons about His Lordship. This decision about marriage to Daniel was to be one more.

And what of her future children? They would live with the consequences of her decision also. Did she prefer a life of ease over a godly father for them? Beth smiled in the dark as she remembered how Daniel had enjoyed meeting the youngest Newmans. His mother had spoken several times of his love for children. Beth knew Daniel believed that God sends children as a gift, perfect in number when planned by Him. How could her future children's mere physical food compare with their spiritual food? To be given a husband who loved God, who followed the Lord and lived out His commandments — there was no comparison at all.

As the visit drew to a close, Beth realized that God had indeed blessed her when He led her parents to Kanesville. By breaking her dependence on her friends and teaching her to be content with only her family around her, He had begun to prepare her for missionary life. Activities like the ones to which she had become accustomed in Tennessee would be in short supply in the Chilean countryside! And they all seemed so unimportant now. The accident, too, had prepared her tremendously. Setting aside her own dreams and desires was a lesson that Beth could see would have to be learned over and over again throughout her lifetime. Jesus was faithful. He had helped her in the past, and He would in the future, as long as she depended on Him. "Without me, ye can do nothing." Beth knew that to be true.

Daniel smiled down at Beth through the open car window as the Grants started their journey home. "I'll write first. And I know I can count on you to write me back as quickly as possible. We'll make the letters fly! I'll be calling again when I figure out when I can come for another visit."

"Remember, I happen to be the correspondence secretary. I know your schedule better than you do. So be sure that it is the first opportunity you have!" laughed Beth. Her eyes shone as she looked at him. Yes, he was definitely worth any changes she had to make in her diet! As they drove away, she already felt a bit lonely for the entire Benton family. When would she see them again?

At home once again, Beth spent the first three days helping her mother. There was unpacking and laundry to do, baking to catch up on, and seeds to plant. Though Beth knew that the mailman could not possibly have a letter for her from

Daniel so soon, it was hard not to hope for one each after-noon. On the fourth day after their arrival home, however, Beth remembered that it was just possible that she could receive a letter from him today, and hurried to the mailbox as soon as she heard the postman's footsteps on the front porch. She was not disappointed. There was an envelope addressed to "Beth Grant, Courtship Correspondent" in a distinctively masculine hand. Beth laughed aloud when she saw the address. Oh, how good God had been to her, to supply Daniel with a sense of humor!

Chapter Seventeen

Beth knew she should put the letter away and read it later. It would show so much self-control and maturity. Besides, it would be nice to be able to think about what the letter might say all day, and then open it in the evening and see if her predictions were true. But, like many a young lady before her, she instead opened it as she walked back into the house.

Seating herself at the desk, she began to read:

May 28

Dear Beth,

It has only been about four hours since you and your family left, but I wanted to write a note to you anyway. It was so nice to see you again. Of course, it was also fun to visit with your family. Before I forget it, please tell them that I enjoyed their visit. And tell John that just after you guys pulled out I found that frog he "lost." It was in the drain tile after all!

Well, you probably know a lot more about me because of your visit! As I sit here writing this letter, I keep wondering: What are her impressions? How is she feeling about this courtship? What questions has she not shared with me? What are her concerns? What positive traits (if any!) has she discovered in me? Is she thinking these same thoughts about me? However, I have to keep telling myself not to jump ahead of God. He will reveal these things to me in His time.

I do think that we made progress in learning more about

each other during your visit. I, for one, can state that the traits I saw in you were positive. I'm especially glad that you didn't try to hide your concerns about living conditions in Chile. The worst thing you (or I) can do during this time of our lives, is to try to hide anything from each other. We must be perfectly candid and frank. I'll try to never withhold any information from you, even if it might not put me in "the best light." Okay?

As I reflected on our discussion about the housing situation in Chile, a few other issues that relate specifically to living in Chile came to mind. I'll jot them down and you can be thinking and praying about them. I'm sure our letters and future visits will allow us plenty of time to discuss them. For now, I'll give you a brief listing of them:

- I think it will be important for you to dress pretty much as the native women dress. Don't worry! It's plenty modest. But, it may not be exactly to your tastes.
- You will need to become quite proficient in the Spanish language. For some people that's a lot to ask. I know you can learn it with the help of God. Also, I would want us to speak Spanish in our home at times, like during meals, so that our children can become bilingual easily.
- All missionaries suffer from a feeling of isolation from parents and friends back home. God is certainly able to help you through those times. Still, you need to know that we couldn't return to the States for every aunt who dies (I am not being flippant when I say that), or after the birth of each of our children. It just can't be done. Of course, we can arrange trips back home for real emergencies and situations, like if one of our parents becomes seriously ill.
- I want to homeschool our children (if God so blesses). I assume that homeschooling, itself, won't be much of a

problem for you since you were home schooled. But, I want to share with you how I would prefer to see it operate in my own home. I'm not big on the use of workbooks; besides, we won't have room in our small house to store lots of stuff. Also, I want to make sure that we cover certain topics. Like Bible knowledge and scripture memory, basic math and grammar (English and Spanish of course!), communication skills, geography, and history. I'm not interested, however, in teaching them things that they will probably never use, like advanced calculus. Does that make sense? What I'm trying to say is that I don't want our homeschooling time to be dictated by what the world thinks is a "proper education." Finally, the homeschooling will not be a set scheduled activity that occurs every day, for example, from 8:45 to 11:50. Missionaries just need to be much more flexible with their schedules.

- Although we would both be considered missionaries (and we would be!) I feel your primary responsibility is to work within the home, raising the children that God might bless us with. You could have Bible studies with some native women, and work alongside me in many ways. But I wouldn't want you to get so involved in the missionary work that our children are neglected. I believe God would place you to serve as a helpmeet to me as I minister to the Chileans and to raise our children. We've not had a chance to discuss this topic before and I hope it won't be a big problem. But, like I said earlier, let's please be honest.

Whew! That's a lot to drop on you in my first letter. Please don't feel overwhelmed. Like I said, we have lots of time to discuss these and other issues that need discussing.

Which brings up an interesting point. What questions do you have for me? What things do I need to be thinking about?

If you feel comfortable writing down some of your thoughts about the issues I've raised, I would love to get your perspective on them. If not, we can just discuss them when I visit you next. Which will be . . . ? I'm not sure. I need to check with my furlough coordinator's correspondence secretary and see what speaking engagements have been lined up . . . So, I'll end this letter for now and look forward to hearing from you.

In Christ,

Daniel

Rejoice evermore. Pray without ceasing. In everything give thanks: for this is the will of God in Christ Jesus concerning you. I Thessalonians 5:16-18

Beth folded the letter and leaned back in the office chair. She realized that she had been sitting on the edge of her seat as she read the letter. Beth could hear the scolding of bluejays outside the open window, but she didn't turn her head to watch them. She had too much to think about right now.

After a few minutes, she unfolded the letter again and reread the contents, slowly this time. Beth tried to picture Daniel sitting at his desk. She could almost see him smiling as he wrote the ending.

Beth now realized that courtship was a serious thing. Oh sure, she had known that it would be important and have long-lasting implications. But she hadn't dreamed it could be as intense as this.

But was this wrong? Was it wrong for Daniel to lay everything out in the open? Was it wrong for him to want to learn how Beth would react to certain situations before they were married? Of course not! The more Beth thought about it, the more committed she was to courtship. What a wonderful method God had provided for two people to make sure that God was leading them together. She shuddered as she thought about the world's way of casual dating with its strong emphasis on romanticism. *It's no wonder that so many marriages end in divorce*, she thought sadly.

Beth got out her writing tablet and started to write Daniel back. She even had his name written on the top of the page. Suddenly, she was struck that this was not the proper way to proceed. She hadn't even prayed about the issues that he had raised. Also, her parents didn't know that she had received this letter. Mom was in the kitchen working on supper, while Dad was out visiting some shut-ins.

Do I really need to share this letter with them? Beth wondered. *It was written to me, and there's nothing in it that Mom or Dad would find offensive or bad.* The more Beth thought about it, the more she didn't like the idea of having every aspect of her life made public. *Why, it wouldn't be fair to Daniel to let them read the letter. He wrote it to me, not them.* And so, Beth continued to convince herself that she should keep this letter a secret.

God, however, must have had other plans, because as the minutes passed, Beth began to feel guilty about not sharing the letter with her parents. As she was struggling with these thoughts, her dad entered the house and walked into the living room.

"Hi, Beth," Dad said. "Where's your mom?"

"I think she's in the kitchen. Did you have a nice visit?"

"Well, yes I did and no I didn't," Dad smiled. "It was good to be an encouragement to Mrs. Vose. She always tells me how much she appreciates my coming by. So I would definitely have to say it was a good visit from that standpoint." He shuffled through the new mail on his desk. "But I couldn't call it a totally nice visit," he mumbled, looking at the mail.

Beth waited for her dad to explain himself, but he got preoccupied with reading an advertisement on the back of an envelope for a new set of books by a religious publisher. Her suspense grew until she couldn't hold it any longer. "Well, what happened, Dad? What was bad about it?"

"Huh?" Dad said, looking absently up at Beth. It was obvious that he had forgotten all about his conversation with her. "Oh, I'm sorry," he said, smiling. "You know that door at Mrs. Vose's house that leads from her porch to the basement? Well, it was left open for some reason and I didn't see it, and . . . well, I guess I sort of ran into it. I was looking to the left at a dog digging in her neighbor's flower bed and ran right smack into it!" He turned his head to show Beth the bruise that was already looking pretty bad.

Beth gasped and said rather loudly, "Oh Dad! I'm so sorry. Are you hurt?"

"I'm okay, Beth. It happened as I was about to knock on her door, so I went ahead and had my visit with her. I really am okay and . . ." He couldn't finish his sentence, though, because Mom came briskly into the room.

"What's wrong, Robert?" she exclaimed. "Didn't I hear Beth say something about your being hurt?" Before he could answer, Mom had already circled Dad and found his bruise. "Honey! What happened?"

Dad went on to tell her about his visit to Mrs. Vose. When everything was calm again, Beth reached down and picked up her letter. "Dad, I got a letter from Daniel today. I would like you and Mom to read it." She handed the letter to Dad.

As Dad reached for the letter, he had a slight frown on his face. "Is everything okay?"

"Yes sir," Beth replied. "I just thought it would be good for you two to read the letters I receive and the ones I send out."

Dad reached over and touched Beth's arm. "You are really maturing, Beth," he said.

"I'm still struggling to mature, Dad," Beth answered honestly.

As Mom and Dad silently read the letter together, Beth watched their faces. What she saw sort of surprised her. Dad began to grin, then smile, then smile even bigger. Mom just had a kind of peaceful look on her face. When they were finished, Dad looked at Mom and nodded.

"What's that all about?" Beth asked her parents, curiously.

"Oh, nothing," Dad said. "Well, have you written him back yet?"

"No sir. I just got his letter about thirty minutes ago. I need time to think about it."

"And pray about it," Dad reminded.

Beth smiled. "You're right, Dad. I need to pray about it, too."

Chapter Eighteen

*D*ear Daniel,

I enjoyed hearing from you very much! It brought back vivid memories of you, as well as of the days spent at your parents' home. I could picture you so well as I read your letter. In every line I seemed to hear even the inflections of your voice.

As I read your letter, I felt so sorry for girls who spend time with a future mate in only recreation and frivolous conversation. I do not for one moment consider myself better than those who follow the world's pattern of dating. I do, however, consider myself far more blessed.

Yes, I can honestly say that I saw many positive traits in you during our visit. I also consider myself very blessed in just knowing you. You have already enriched my life and challenged me to a closer walk with the Savior. And yes, I know that sooner or later, I'll see that you aren't perfect! (I think you already know that about me.) But just knowing that you are being as honest and open as possible with me reassures me. I'll be a bit relieved, I think, to know that you are human.

As I read over the list of topics for me to think and pray about, an important point occurred to me. I should let you know, first of all, that it is my desire to be a submissive wife. Most girls involved in a courtship would probably say the same thing! But I want you to know that this is much more than mere lip-service to a much talked-about issue.

I don't think I ever told you, but I spent the better part of two years struggling with the issue of submission to my father.

I really did struggle. During that time, I would have said that I was a submissive daughter, but I was not truly submissive at all. I was outwardly obedient, but inwardly resentful that we moved here from Tennessee. I was not blatantly rebellious, but I see now that an independent, "Why can't I do as I please?" spirit is still rebellion, no matter how one tries to hide it.

The Lord used my accident, as well as a few other situations, to teach me the real meaning of submission. My Heavenly Father wants me to submit myself to Him first, and to then submit myself to whomever He places in authority over me. If it is His will for you to become my husband, then you will become that authority.

What am I trying to say? I do not consider our courtship, and later possible engagement, to be a time of negotiation. I do not wish to "cut the best deal that I can" before our marriage. It is my heart's desire to approach our relationship as a "wife in training" — to try to understand your expectations and wishes for our future home and life together. If the Lord should show one or both of us, or our parents, that our marriage is not His will, then I must accept that. But I will not try to change you into who I want you to be, before or after our marriage. I know this will be hard to resist, because it is a weakness women have! But I am depending on the power of the Holy Spirit to help me.

With that in mind, I will respond to each of the topics you mentioned. I am not trying to argue any points here — I accept the fact that you have a right to decide these things — but I do need some clarification.

Just how do the native women dress? You said it was "plenty modest." Could you elaborate? Dresses and/or skirts, I hope? How long? Do you have any pictures? I really need some specifics. And would I need those things before my arrival in Chile? Am I ever thankful that I learned to sew!

What is "proficient" in the Spanish language? I have a feeling that languages will be hard for me, although I don't really know. Michael spoke Portuguese with ease the last time he was here, and very rapidly, I might add. It was quite impressive! Of course it probably helped that he learned some as a child in Brazil. I hope you are patient! I do promise to try hard.

Isolation from my family will be very difficult, probably the most difficult thing of all. I have spent the past three years, for the most part, in the company of only my family. They have become my best friends. I believe that is what God wanted of me for the last three years. If He is now asking me to leave them behind, I know His grace is sufficient. But I am afraid it will be a real struggle. I am glad you would be there to help me.

Homeschooling — how thankful I am that you are committed to homeschooling. Perhaps a discussion of that would work best on your next visit. I have so much to ask you about that subject. I tend to be a very scheduled person. I can certainly understand the need to be flexible as a missionary, and I can see that is another area in which the Lord will have many lessons to teach me. And not just about homeschooling, I'm sure! I suppose that I will have to learn to be flexible about everything imaginable. I need some help imagining what those things might be.

I am thankful for your view of a missionary's wife. Even though my mom was a missionary before her marriage, when she married Dad, her role changed drastically. After she read your letter, she remembered that your parents held the same view. How glad I am that we are all in agreement on that point!

Now, do I have questions for you? Yes! Many! Most of them I hope to ask in person very soon. If it is possible for you to get here, the week of July 10 is free for you, as is the week following (July 17), and the weekend between those two weeks. Any time in that opening is fine with Mom and Dad (and me — and I don't have to tell you how fine it is with John and Adam!). Let us know when to expect you.

And just to get you started thinking, there are a few questions that are weighing heavily on my mind. In your letter, you said that you felt my primary role was to "work within the home, raising the children that God might bless us with." I agree! That's biblical. And I would be very happy with that. But, what exactly do you mean by "raise the children?" What responsibilities are mine? Would they be pretty much mine alone? Do you see us as not being together much of the time? I know that missionaries can lead very busy lives, and that you have begun missionary service as a single man. Do you see yourself continuing to keep the same schedule? Will I be primarily responsible for the spiritual upbringing of our children? Would we have much time together as a family? This is of great concern to me, and I do need you to be quite open and honest. Perhaps you are not sure yourself of the answers yet — these are probably not the kinds of questions that you have turned over in your mind as a single missionary. Please do now, though!

I am looking forward to hearing from you again soon. And seeing you again will be even better. Please tell your parents that the Grant family sends much love. Your parents are very special people.

Your Courtship Correspondent and Furlough Advisor,

Beth

Chapter Nineteen

Beth waited for a reply from Daniel, but it was about a week and a half before another envelope addressed to "Beth Grant, Courtship Correspondent" arrived in her family's mailbox. Dad brought it in with the rest of the mail. "Here's a letter for you, ma'am," he said, smiling at Beth. Since she was busy kneading bread dough, she had no choice but to wait a few minutes before opening it.

"Well, what's the news from Chicago?" Dad asked as Beth finished reading the letter. "I hope all is going well?"

"Yes, things seem to be going well in Chicago, Dad," Beth sighed. "Here, you can read it." She handed the letter to her dad.

Dear Beth,

I received your letter a few days ago and have been so busy I didn't have time to respond right away. Sorry! I'll try to do better.

I liked the tone of your letter and the fact that you asked me questions also. Now we're really opening up. I like that!

I would love to write down my comments about your questions to me, but after praying about it I've decided that it would be best to discuss them in person. I hope that is okay with you.

Speaking of "in person," how does July 14-16 sound to the Grants for a visit from Daniel Benton? According to my furlough coordinator's correspondence secretary I have that time free. Let me know. And, keep thinking of questions you might want to ask me.

Daniel

P.S. This is fun and potentially very rewarding, too! Don't you think?

"Well, that sounds like a good letter to me, Beth," Dad said. "What's wrong?"

"Oh, it's nothing, really. It's just that I wish he would have told me what he thought of my concerns, that's all."

Dad leaned on the end of the table. "Don't you think that's really up to Daniel to decide? I mean, he did pray about it and apparently had a good reason for wanting to talk about it with you in person."

Beth could do nothing but agree with her dad. "I know. I guess I'm just impatient, Dad."

"I understand," Dad said softly. He patted her arm and said, "I'll pray that God will give you patience in this matter."

Beth looked at her dad, then smiled and nodded, indicating that she appreciated both his concern and his promise to pray for her.

Time slipped by for Beth, and before long July 14th rolled around on the calendar. "Today's the day!" the excited boys shouted as they saw Beth for the first time that morning.

When Daniel arrived at the Grants' front door, he was met with the usual flurry of activity and announcements. John and Adam had much to fill him in on, and Daniel patiently and willingly listened to their long report, even though his luggage was still sitting beside him.

After a few minutes, John and Adam raced off to find a treasure to share with Daniel—it happened to be a box of spent shotgun shells that a neighbor had shared with them. While they were gone, Beth exchanged friendly greetings with Daniel and offered to get him a glass of iced tea. While standing in the kitchen, Beth noticed the calendar by the phone. "Daniel, I'm so glad you could come this weekend.

It's a pretty special one to our family. You see, every year we go to the county fair. Our family has always made a day of this. There are lots of displays of fruits, vegetables, jams, animals, quilts, everything. We get there early, meet some of the people we know, eat lunch on the grounds, and well, just have a great time. I was hoping you would want to go and meet some of our friends. They are excited about the chance to meet you."

Rather than being excited, Daniel seemed disappointed. *Now, what's wrong with a county fair?* Beth thought to herself.

Daniel seemed to be choosing his words carefully. He smiled, took another gulp of tea, then began. "Beth, I wouldn't do anything in the world to hurt your feelings or spoil your fun. Although I've never been to a county fair, it sounds like it could be fun. But . . ." and then he paused. "But . . . you know we just don't have that much time to talk together. We have a lot to talk about these next few days. I don't want to disappoint you or your family. I guess I'm not sure what to say," he finally said.

Beth stood still looking at Daniel. She wanted to say, "Why can't we go? How much time would it take?" But she didn't say those things. Instead, she just stood quietly looking at him.

After a minute, Daniel began again, "I'm sorry, Beth. I can see that this is a big deal for you. If you want to spend our time together at a county fair, I suppose we could. It's just that I feel we need to be a bit more judicious with the time that God has allowed us to be together. We have so much to talk about." As Daniel finished, Dad walked into the room.

After greetings were exchanged, Dad stated, "Well, you sure are going to be busy on this visit, Daniel. I guess Beth has already told you we have this county fair . . ."

Before Dad could finish, Beth interjected, "Dad, Daniel

and I aren't sure we should go to the county fair. I'm sorry for interrupting you, but we've been talking about it and we both feel that it would be best for us to spend our time more wisely. We don't have much opportunity to talk, you know."

Dad smiled. "That's okay with me. Going to be too hot for me, anyway. I think Betty and I will be glad to stay home this year." As he walked out of the room, Dad noticed a grin on Daniel's face. Beth had one, too.

The visit was a productive one for Daniel and Beth. They talked about many issues and concerns that each had. Daniel had brought some more pictures of how the women dressed in Chile, which relieved any fears that Beth might have. She decided that she would have no problem dressing in the same way as the native women.

During a long talk on the front porch, the two discussed the important issue of time management. "I'm afraid that for the last six years or so, each of my 24 hours has been mine to spend any way I pleased to spend them. Don't get me wrong! I haven't spent my time playing or goofing off. It's just that I can work on a sermon at 9:00 in the morning, at 2:00 in the middle of the night, or while eating supper, depending on when it makes the most sense for me." Daniel picked up a leaf that had blown onto the porch from the strong thunderstorm the night before, and studied its structure as he formed his thoughts into words. "I'm sure the Lord will teach me how to order my days as a husband."

"You said in one of your letters that you felt my primary role was to 'work within the home, raising the children that God might bless us with.' What role do you see for yourself in the raising of our children?" Beth asked. "I know you plan on taking a role, but what would that role be?" She was so thankful she could be candid and forthright with Daniel. Still, she was anxious to hear his answer.

"If God blesses us with a family, then God would also

give me the primary responsibility to see that my children are brought up in the nurture and admonition of the Lord. I would be the one that the Lord would hold responsible for that, not you. Of course, circumstances might dictate that I have to delegate certain things to you at times. For example, if I have to make a trip into the city with a sick villager, I would expect you to read the Bible with the children, pray with them, and keep up with their study of scriptures. But, I don't expect you to carry the majority of the load nor the responsibility of raising the family," he concluded.

Beth was pleased with his answer. It was calming to hear him use the words, "It is my responsibility." The more she thought about it, the more the issue seemed resolved. Daniel would be the spiritual leader of their family, just as Dad had been when she was growing up.

Later in the day, however, Beth began to have some concerns about Daniel's answer. What was that he had said, "If I have to make a trip into the city . . ."? She had heard him talk about making such trips before. But how big a problem would this be?

Beth didn't like the unsettled feelings she was having. So, after supper, she asked Daniel, "How often do you make trips to the city? How long will you be gone at a time? I just don't want there to be any surprises."

Daniel agreed. "I don't want there to be any surprises, either. But, I'm sorry that I won't be able to give you many specifics on this one. You see, it's impossible for me to know how many trips I will take or how long each one will last. If you are ever there, I think you will see pretty quickly why it is so hard to pin down something like this. I do make plans. Daily, weekly, and monthly plans. But these can change completely in a matter of moments. For example, I had the opportunity to take one of the villagers into Antofagasta for emergency surgery about three months before I returned to the States. This man was actually hostile to my work and what I represent. Yet, during that trip I was able to show him the love of Christ and offer a testimony for Jesus. For that specific trip, I was gone for three days. How often does that happen? Well, I may go for two months without such a trip, and then have two trips like that in a single week. There's just no way to predict. I'm sorry."

"I think I understand," Beth answered softly. Still, it was hard for her to calculate the impact of these trips on her possible future life as Daniel's wife. She changed her focus. "What would our family life be like in those times when emergencies don't come up?"

Daniel smiled at Beth. He knew she was serious about his involvement in raising their children. And he was glad for it. "Well, here's the way I hope it will be with a family, assuming no emergencies. I would try my best to be home every evening. I also want you to know that I will be responsible for the spiritual training of our family. I would be sure to lead the family in daily Bible reading, scripture memory, and prayer. It would be my primary responsibility to lead discussions of character traits. I would be involved in this on a daily basis, unless of course I am not physically present. Does that answer your question?"

Beth's eyes were shining. "Yes, that answers my question, Daniel." It seemed to Beth that God was blessing her in a special way.

The visit continued to include many talks. Talks which included Beth's parents at times. Through it all, Beth and Daniel were always in the company of someone else. Beth didn't think this was strange at all and was thankful for the purity that the arrangement kept in their courtship. *Why would anyone want it any other way?* she thought to herself.

All too soon, the visit ended. Both promised to write soon, and Daniel said he would write her first. As he drove down the street, Beth turned and sat down on the porch with her parents. They began to talk about Daniel's visit and what Beth had learned. These talks had been occurring all along, and were a way for Beth and her parents to keep a pulse on the status of the courtship. How grateful she was that she had parents who cared about her and were always there for her.

After hearing about Daniel's plan for spiritual leadership in his home, Dad turned to Beth. "I'm glad you had a good visit. Your mother and I are very impressed with Daniel. We have given the matter much prayer, as I am sure you have as well. I've also had a few conversations with his parents." He paused. It wasn't like Dad to have to search for words. "What I mean to say is this: if Daniel should decide that the Lord is leading him to marry you, you have our blessing." Dad was smiling, yet Mom had tears in her eyes.

"Mom, is everything okay? Is anything wrong?" Beth asked.

"Oh no, Beth," Mom reassured her. "Everything is fine. I'm in full agreement. It's just that I was thinking about how young you are. You're only nineteen years old. Of course, you'll be twenty in January," she added, smiling through her tears. "I just wasn't expecting this so soon, that's all. I am truly glad to give my daughter to someone who loves the Lord so much, and whom I already love as a son."

Dad added, "There's no particular age at which someone is ready for marriage. I know some would say that you have to be twenty-five or something like that. But honestly, Beth, we believe that when the Lord leads someone to marry you and it is obviously His will, we shouldn't question Him. You need to be mature to take such a step. Some girls aren't mature even at twenty-five! But your mother and I have prayed about this and feel you are mature enough to make this step, if it is His will."

Beth wasn't quite prepared for this talk. With a quavering voice she asked softly, "Has Daniel asked you if he could marry me?"

"No, Beth, he hasn't asked us yet," Dad replied honestly. "All we are saying is that, if he should, the answer he will get from us is that we approve."

During the next few weeks, Beth frequently thought about the past conversations she had had with her parents and Daniel. Also, the two started writing each other more frequently. In one of Daniel's letters, he stated:

". . . I was thinking about our discussion of what the women in Chile wear. I hope you also have considered what it would be like to live in the dry climate there. To help you understand more about life there, I've enclosed a couple of pamphlets and some letters I wrote home to my folks, which highlight what it is like to live there every day. Also, I've sent a list of books that will tell you more about Chile and the area . . . I must admit it took even me some getting used to, but I am quite fond of it in its own way now. There are some spectacular landscapes. Atacama is the most arid desert . . ."

This gave Beth more to think about. How would she like living in a desert? She honestly didn't know!

As the letters continued, a date was chosen in which Beth would come to Chicago for a visit at the Benton home. " . . . So, it looks like we are all ready for your visit on August 12-14. I'll try to practice grilling out hamburgers and have my style perfected by the time you arrive . . ." Daniel wrote.

I wonder what this visit will bring, thought Beth as she held Daniel's letter. God knew and it was in His hands.

Chapter Twenty

ood morning, little lady. Plenty of seats right up in front, if you like. And I'll take that for you." The gray-haired bus driver smiled at Beth as he reached for her suitcase.

Beth gratefully returned the older man's smile and gave him her suitcase. Maybe riding the bus to Chicago wouldn't be so bad after all. It certainly had not been her idea. But Dad felt that it would be a good experience for her. If she married Daniel, she was sure to encounter less than ideal traveling arrangements at some point in her life. And although Beth wasn't really enthusiastic about riding this bus, she had to admit that it was quite a bit easier to begin on this one, rather than one of those busses that she recalled seeing in rural South America. *At least I don't have a lady sitting next to me with a chicken on her lap and a burrito in her hand*, she reflected. *Maybe someday I will, though!* Beth smiled to herself.

In the Chicago terminal, Beth heard a familiar voice behind her. "Miss Grant I believe?" Beth turned to see Daniel's smiling face, and she had to laugh as he swept a cap off his head with a slight bow. "Your carriage awaits."

"At least, I hope it awaits! This is Chicago you know!" added Randy Benton. "Let's find Beth's suitcase and get her home, son." Beth was only too glad to walk with Daniel and his father out to their car. This bus terminal was a much larger and busier place than the tiny Kanesville depot. So many strange people were there--some of them very strange indeed. *I'd definitely prefer the lady with the chicken on her lap!* thought Beth.

Later that evening, in the peace and safety of the Benton home, Daniel handed Beth a small package. The opened box revealed a set of teaching tapes in the Spanish language. "I thought you might like to take these home with you," Daniel explained. "You don't have to worry about passing a test or anything! But maybe it will give you some idea of what you would be getting into."

"Thank you . . . I think! I know it's probably silly of me, but I kind of dread this. I just know that it will be very difficult for me," worried Beth. Turning to Mrs. Benton, she asked, "Was learning Spanish hard for you? You even had a couple of children before you became a missionary, and not much time to study. But you learned it without too much trouble, didn't you?" Beth finished hopefully.

Mrs. Benton smiled sympathetically and shook her head. "I'm sorry to disappoint you Beth, if you were looking to me for reassurance! I really did have difficulty learning a foreign language." Seeing Beth's woeful expression, Mrs. Benton added hastily, "I did learn it, though. It just took some time. And time certainly was in short supply with two young children, and the Lord adding two more in just a few years."

Margaret Benton gazed thoughtfully across the room, then returned her eyes to Beth's. "You know, I believe my biggest problem in learning the language was myself. I felt that I had to learn it, in my own strength, as soon as possible. When I finally gave up in frustration, the Lord was able to teach me the meaning of His strength being perfected in my weakness. Every day I found it easier to communicate with the people around me, when I focused on the people themselves. I gave their needs and lives a higher priority than learning the language, and God honored that."

Beth sat in silence for a moment. "Thank you so much," she reflected. "I'll try to remember that. And I would appreciate your prayers. I need to trust that if the Lord calls me there, He'll teach me anything I need to know."

The patio seemed an ideal place for breakfast on Wednesday morning. The humidity from the day before had been dispersed by a thunderstorm during the night, and the air was dry and pleasant. The sun shone warmly on the little group around the table, as they bowed their heads in thanks for the food set before them.

"Beth, you once mentioned that you are a very scheduled person. I've noticed some very positive things in that character trait. You always seem to be organized, and ready for every responsibility. Meals that you cook are always on time, and no one ever says things like, 'Isn't she <u>ever</u> going to be ready?'" Daniel exaggerated his voice a bit, and everyone laughed. "I really do appreciate those qualities. But perhaps we need to discuss how those same traits could work against you on the mission field." He hesitated, then smiled cheerfully at Beth. "Do you feel ready to tackle that this morning?"

Beth blushed, then laughed. "I suppose if I don't answer 'yes' to that question, I'll appear to be either a coward or conceited! But yes, I honestly do feel ready."

"I'm sorry," Daniel said apologetically. "I didn't mean to put you on the spot. I just feel we should talk as many things through as possible, and I tend to be a very direct, matter-of-fact person. I hope you can get used to that!"

"I think I can," Beth assured him. "I like your honesty and directness very much. At least I should always know where I stand!" she finished.

"Good," Daniel approved. "Now, first of all, as you think ahead to the possibility of life on the mission field, you will have to put all ideas of strict schedules completely out of your head. Things seldom work exactly according to plans, no matter how carefully laid those plans may be. I'm not talking here about utter chaos. I do make plans. But I try to never let the plan obscure the goal."

Beth's eyes twinkled. "I remember you told me that your plans often change at a moment's notice. Did you have some tips for me, to help me prepare for that kind of a life?"

"I'm not sure if I would call them tips, exactly," Daniel smiled. "But I do think that this idea of flexibility instead of having one's own agenda will be very important to you. Take homeschooling our children, for example. Education is, in my opinion, not an end in itself. It is simply a means by which we can prepare our children to love and serve God. The basis for making decisions about what we should teach them must be — 'will this help them to bring glory to God?'

"I want my children to be able to read God's Word. As Paul wrote, 'Study to show thyself approved unto God, a workman that needeth not to be ashamed, rightly dividing the word of truth.' We need to remember that they are to study to be approved by God, not necessarily by men. I would want to see them first learn to love and serve others, and to help us in our work. The other things that I mentioned in my first letter can be taught as we find time."

"That's understandable," replied Beth. "I can certainly see what you mean." She shifted a bit in the patio chair. Her leg was beginning to ache from sitting in the low seat. Daniel noticed it, and had a suggestion.

"Why don't we take a walk? I want to keep myself in good shape while I'm on furlough. I do so much walking at home in Chile — I certainly don't want the villagers laughing at me when I go home!"

Beth smiled at Daniel as she stood up. "That's a great idea. My leg gives me trouble if I sit in one position for a long period of time. Walking is something I really enjoy."

"Good!" Daniel was pleased. "That's something we can enjoy together, anywhere we may be." As they started off down the street, the older Bentons followed behind, strolling contentedly in the sunshine. Daniel set a brisk pace. A very brisk pace. It was so brisk that Beth quickly fell behind. Anyone with full use of their legs would have been hard-pressed to keep up with Daniel Benton's stride, and Beth didn't have full use of her left leg. Daniel continued to march right along, completely unaware that Beth was not beside him. His face was away from her, watching children splashing in a small plastic pool. Beth was too embarrassed to call out to him, and hoped he would soon see that she had fallen behind. Eventually he did notice. "I'm sorry!" he exclaimed. "Was I walking that fast? I do like a brisk walk."

"It's my leg," Beth explained shyly. "I'm just not able to walk really fast. I enjoy walking very much, but, well, I didn't realize that I walked so slowly." Inwardly she added, *Poor guy. Here you like to walk briskly, and now you may marry me and be stuck plodding through life, just to be nice.*

Daniel noticed Beth's unhappy expression. Facing her, he waited for her eyes to meet his. "Beth, what's the matter? We're having a lovely walk on a beautiful morning. Why are you suddenly unhappy?" As Beth hesitated, unsure of how she should answer him, Daniel added, "Remember, we promised to be totally honest with each other. Now tell me why you are unhappy," he finished firmly.

Beth was surprised by the firmness in his voice. Looking up, however, she saw only concern in his face. "I was just thinking . . . well, I was thinking that you said you like a brisk walk, and that's impossible for me. You had said earlier that walking was something we would be able to enjoy together. I just feel bad that you won't be able to really enjoy walking, if you walk with me. I'll be a hindrance to you." Her eyes began to fill with tears in spite of her efforts to stop them.

Daniel saw the tears, but didn't seem too upset by them. "Beth, it's no big deal. Really. I like to walk briskly, but you can't. That's just the way it's going to be. I'd much prefer a

slower walk with you than a brisk one alone." He waited for
her to reply, but she was unable. Finding a tissue in the pocket
of her skirt, she hastily dried the tears that had escaped her
eyes and were making their way down her cheeks. After
waiting a moment, he continued. "Are you embarrassed about
your leg, Beth? I didn't think it bothered you. You didn't
seem sensitive about it at all when I met you."

"I guess that was before I had any idea that you could
someday become my husband," Beth answered in a shaky
voice. "I thought I had given all of my concerns about my leg
to the Lord, but maybe I've been trying to take them back
lately."

"I see," Daniel said gently, and this time Beth looked up
into a face filled with kindness. "Come on, let's walk a bit
more, and I'll try to explain something to you." As they
continued down the street, Daniel looked over at his companion. "Beth, I want you to know that your leg is not an issue.
It doesn't matter to me that you are unable to walk fast. It
doesn't matter to me that you limp. I suppose that your leg
may be scarred, or disfigured in some way, but that doesn't
bother me either. If the Lord is truly leading us together,
Beth, He is not doing it based on what we look like, or how
smart we are, or any one of a number of other things that
sometimes attract people to each other. If He is leading us
together, it is because He wants to use our marriage to bring
honor and glory and praise to His Name, in some way. Our
lives together can have no place for fear. I will gratefully
accept you as you are, and even as you will become in the
future. One day we will both be old, and it will not happen
overnight. Day by day we will grow toward old age. Never
be afraid that I will be sorry that I married you, no matter
what accident or disease may befall you. If you are God's
choice for me, you will always be His choice for me, as long
as you live. I trust His wisdom completely. So must you."

Chapter Twenty-one

ix days after Beth's return to Kanesville, Daniel received a letter from his "courtship correspondent." The envelope was dark blue, as was the stationery inside. At the top of the page were written the words:

Have I Got The Blues!

Dear Daniel,

As you may have guessed, I have been listening to the Spanish tapes. I tried my best to learn some of the phrases. But I believe that I will have to be taught by the same instructor as your mom was — the Holy Spirit. (I'm not really blue about that. What better teacher could I have?) . . .

Here is the recipe your mom asked for. Tell her that it will work just as well with frozen strawberries. We use whole wheat flour and really like it that way . . .

I have prayed a lot this week about becoming more flexible in my daily life. I realize that no matter what the outcome of this courtship may be, I need to see my days in a different light. The Lord can use me best if I let Him plan my days. I still have things that I would like to accomplish each day, but I am striving to be cheerful if things do not work out as I had hoped. I'm afraid that I have probably had a great deal of pride in this area — I know that I have organizational skills, and I am very detail oriented. Like learning Spanish, it will take the Holy Spirit to teach me how to be more responsive to the Lord's leading. Please pray for me. It is so nice to know that I can depend on you to do that. My dad was voted "Most Dependable" by his high school senior class. I think that would be a good title for you, too . . .

So the weekend of September 5th sounds good to us. We're all looking forward to seeing you. Adam and John have something cooked up between them, I'm not sure what. Those two are really glad that you came into our lives. So is their sister.

See you then. I pray for you daily.

Hasta luego,
Beth

September arrived in Kanesville. It was still warm although the heat of the summer seemed to have finally broken. The nights were cooler and there was just a suggestion in the air that fall could be somewhere in the general vicinity. Beth waited anxiously for the 5th to arrive.

The family sat on the front porch one evening, enjoying the cool breeze. Dad talked to Mom about how pleased he was with the way things were going at Grace Mission. God had certainly blessed his humble efforts at organizing an evangelical church in Kanesville. While the numbers were growing steadily, Dad was happier that he could see signs of spiritual growth among the members. They were beginning to demonstrate the true test of believers found in John 13:35: "By this shall all men know that ye are my disciples, if ye have love one to another."

"When is Daniel coming, Beth?" John asked.

"In a few days," Beth replied. "I hope the weather stays nice like it is now for his visit."

"Me too," echoed Adam. "Maybe he can go down to the creek with us and try to catch some fish!"

"Maybe," Beth laughed. "We'll just have to wait and see what the weather is like."

September 5th arrived with an accompanying downpour. The gutters were overflowing and the street had large puddles in it. The house seemed stuffy since the windows had to be closed almost all the way to keep the rain from rushing into the house. *Well, there goes our hope for a nice day,* thought Beth as she washed the breakfast dishes.

Yet, as the morning progressed, the rain slowed down and stopped completely about ten o'clock. The clouds were moving rapidly, and a beautiful rainbow arched the sky. Dad opened the windows and a fresh, clean fragrance filled the house.

Daniel arrived right after lunch and was greeted as always with wild enthusiasm from John and Adam. "Say, do you want to go to the creek and try to catch some fish?" John asked, almost as soon as Daniel entered the house.

"Hold on there, guys! Let a man get his bearings first, okay? Let me settle in here and I'll get back to you. For now, why don't you guys go and see if you can round up some worms for bait?"

At that, the boys were off, flipping over rocks and logs, looking for large worms. There were plenty to find, thanks to the heavy rains.

Even though Daniel claimed he had eaten lunch, Mom fixed him a snack in the kitchen. Daniel obediently ate it while telling Dad, Mom, and Beth what had happened in the past few weeks. After his snack was finished, everyone headed outdoors to enjoy the beauty of the day.

As Mom and Dad walked out to the yard, admiring the worms the boys had found, Daniel sat next to Beth on the porch steps. Daniel turned to Beth and lowered his voice. "Three years ago, I began making a special request of the Lord. I asked Him to bring a wife to me, just as He brought Rebekah to Isaac. Beth, you are my 'Rebekah.' Would you honor me by becoming my wife?"

"Daniel Josiah Benton, I would be honored to be your wife," Beth whispered.

Chapter Twenty-two

It was a clear, cold November morning. It was not, however, just any morning. This was a wedding day. Slowly Beth opened her eyes. The little bedroom that had been hers for more than three years came into focus, as Beth reflected back over the past. It was hard to believe now that a large and pretty bedroom had ever been important to her. How blessed she felt just to have a roof over her head, especially when she remembered the words of the Lord Jesus. "The foxes have holes, and the birds of the air have nests; but the Son of man hath not where to lay his head."

She had once resented this tiny room, but how she had grown to love it. God had taught her many lessons in quiet hours spent here. First during the months of homesickness for Tennessee, then later as she grew to accept His will for her life. The time of recuperation following the accident, and many struggles of giving up "self" had taken place in this little room. She would miss it, just as she would miss the rest of this small and creaky old house. Beth smiled to herself. If only she could have seen ahead! She wouldn't have struggled so.

No, thought Beth. *God knows best. He doesn't let us see the future, because it is best for us not to know what will come, good or bad. He wants us to trust Him for the future, without any guarantees of happiness.* She would not have had to grow as a Christian if she had known everything would turn out so wonderfully. God wanted her to give up all her dreams, and willingly become the woman He molded her into. "And He isn't finished with me yet," she added aloud. A tiny bit of fear crept into her heart as she realized that He would continue to mold her in the future. It was not likely that she would enjoy all of the lessons He still had for her.

Beth slipped out of her bed to kneel beside it. "What time I am afraid, I will trust in Thee," Beth prayed. "Help me, Father, not to be afraid. Help me to remember the lessons I have already learned. You are all wise, and You can be trusted. You will never leave me nor forsake me. Please help me to be the wife You would have me to be. Help me to be submissive, and to learn the lessons You still have for me quickly, so that You do not have to make me repeat them. Thank You, thank You, dear Father, for the wonderful gifts You have given to me. My parents, my brothers, and the home in which You allowed me to be raised, a Christian home. And Daniel. Thank You so much for Daniel. Thank You for his parents, and the home that he was raised in, one that honors You. Thank You for the work You have given him. Help me to be a true helpmeet. Go with us today, and help us to trust You as we begin our new lives together. Prepare the hearts of the people you have sent us to, and help us to be a light in the darkness there. Please keep us in Your care. Keep our parents in Your care, while we are apart. And grant that we may one day meet safe on the other shore. Thank you, dear Heavenly Father, for helping me to wait for my Isaac. In Jesus' Name, Amen."

And they called Rebekah, and said unto her, Wilt thou go with this man? And she said, I will go . . . And Isaac went out to meditate in the field at the eventide: and he lifted up his eyes, and saw, and, behold, the camels were coming. And Rebekah lifted up her eyes, and when she saw Isaac, she lighted off the camel . . . And Isaac brought her into his mother Sarah's tent, and took Rebekah, and she became his wife; and he loved her . . .

The End

Castleberry Farms Press

Our primary goal in publishing is to provide wholesome books in a manner that brings honor to our Lord. We believe in setting no evil thing before our eyes (Psalm 101:3) and although there are many outstanding books, we have had trouble finding enough good reading material for our children. Therefore, we feel the Lord has led us to start this family business.

We believe the following: The Bible is the infallible true Word of God. That God is the Creator and Controller of the universe. That Jesus Christ is the only begotten Son of God, born of the virgin Mary, lived a perfect life, was crucified, buried, rose again, sits at the right hand of God, and makes intercession for the saints. That Jesus Christ is the only Savior and way to the Father. That salvation is based on faith alone, but true faith will produce good works. That the Holy Spirit is given to believers as Guide and Comforter. That the Lord Jesus will return again. That man was created to glorify God and enjoy Him forever.

We began writing and publishing in mid-1996 and hope to add more books in the future if the Lord is willing. All books are written by Mr. and Mrs. Castleberry.

We would love to hear from you if you have any comments or suggestions. Our address is at the end of this section. Now, we'll tell you a little about our books.

The Courtship Series

These books are written to encourage those who intend to follow a Biblically-based courtship that includes the active involvement of parents. The main characters are committed followers of Jesus Christ, and Christian family values are emphasized throughout. The reader will be encouraged to heed parental advice and to live in obedience to the Lord.

Jeff McLean: His Courtship

Follow the story of Jeff McLean as he seeks God's direction for his life. This book is the newest in our courtship series, and is written from a young man's perspective. A discussion of godly traits to seek in young men and women is included as part of the story. February 1998. ISBN 1-891907-05-0. Paperback. $7.50 (plus shipping and handling).

The Courtship of Sarah McLean

Sarah McLean is a nineteen year-old girl who longs to become a wife and mother. The book chronicles a period of two years, in which she has to learn to trust her parents and God fully in their decisions for her future. Paperback, 2nd printing, 1997. ISBN 1-891907-00-X. $7.50 (plus shipping and handling).

Waiting for Her Isaac

Sixteen year-old Beth Grant is quite happy with her life and has no desire for any changes. But God has many lessons in store before she is ready for courtship. The story of Beth's spiritual journey toward godly woman-hood is told along with the story of her courtship. Paperback. 1997. ISBN 1-891907-03-4. $7.50 (plus shipping and handling).

The Farm Mystery Series

Join Jason and Andy as they try to solve the mysterious happenings on the Nelson family's farm. These are books that the whole family will enjoy. In fact, many have used them as read-aloud-to-the-family books. Parents can be assured that there are no murders or other objectionable elements in these books. The boys learn lessons in obedience and responsibility while having lots of fun. There are no worldly situations or language, and no boy-girl relationships. Just happy and wholesome Christian family life, with lots of everyday adventure woven in.

Footprints in the Barn

Who is the man in the green car? What is going on in the hayloft? Is there something wrong with the mailbox? And what's for lunch? The answers to these and many other interesting questions are found in the book Footprints in the Barn. Hardcover. 1996. ISBN 1-891907-01-8. $12 (plus shipping and handling).

The Mysterious Message

The Great Detective Agency is at it once again, solving mysteries on the Nelson farmstead. Why is there a pile of rocks in the woods? Is someone stealing gas from the mill? How could a railroad disappear? And will Jason and Andy have to eat biscuits without honey? You will have to read this second book in the Farm Mystery Series to find out. Paperback. 1997. ISBN 1-891907-04-2. $7.50 (plus shipping and handling).

Midnight Sky

What is that sound in the woods? Has someone been

stealing Dad's tools? Why is a strange dog barking at midnight? And will the Nelsons be able to adopt Russian children? <u>Midnight Sky</u> provides the answers. Paperback. 1998. ISBN 1-891907-06-9. $7.50 (plus shipping and handling).

Other Books

Our Homestead Story: The First Years

The true and humorous account of one family's journey toward a more self-sufficient life-style with the help of God. Read about our experiences with cows, chickens, horses, sheep, gardening and more. Paperback. 1996. ISBN 1-891907-02-6. $7.50 (plus shipping and handling).

Call Her Blessed

This book is designed to encourage mothers to consistently, day by day, follow God's will in their role as mothers. Examples are provided of mothers who know how to nurture and strengthen their children's faith in God. Paperback. 1998. ISBN 1-891907-08-5. $6.00 (plus shipping and handling).

The Orchard Lane Series: In the Spring of the Year

Meet the Hunter family and share in their lives as they move to a new home. The first in our newest series, <u>In the Spring of the Year</u> is written especially for children ages 5-10. Nancy, Caleb, and Emily learn about obedience and self-denial while enjoying the simple pleasures of innocent childhood. Paperback. 1999. ISBN 1-891907-07-7. $8.00 (plus shipping and handling).

The Delivery

Joe Reynolds is a husband and father striving to live a life pleasing to the Lord Jesus Christ. Having been a Christian only seven years, he has many questions and challenges in his life. How does a man working in the world face temptation? How doe he raise his family in a Christ-honoring way? This book attempts to Biblically address many of the issues that men face daily, in a manner that will not cause the reader to stumble in his walk with the Lord. The book is written for men (and young men) by a man – we ask men to read it first, before reading it aloud to their families. Paperback. 1999. ISBN 1-891907-09-3. $9.00 (plus shipping and handling).

Shipping and Handling Costs

The shipping and handling charge is $2.00 for the first book and 50¢ for each additional book you buy in the same order.

You can save on shipping by getting an order together with your friends or homeschool group. On orders of 10-24 books, shipping is only 50¢ per book. Orders of 25 or more books are shipped FREE. Just have each person write a check for their own total, send in all the checks, and indicate **one** address for shipping.

To order, please send a check for the total, including shipping (Wisconsin residents, please add 5.5% sales tax on the total, including shipping and handling charges) to:

Castleberry Farms Press
Dept. TD
P.O. Box 337
Poplar, WI 54864

Please note that prices and shipping charges are subject to change.

CASTLEBERRY FARMS PRESS
P.O. BOX 337
POPLAR, WI 54864

Description	Quantity	Unit Price	Total
The Courtship of Sarah McLean		$7.50	
Waiting for Her Isaac		$7.50	
Jeff McLean: His Courtship		$7.50	
Footprints in the Barn (hardback)		$12.00	
The Mysterious Message		$7.50	-
Midnight Sky		$7.50	
Our Homestead Story		$7.50	
Call Her Blessed		$6.00	
In the Spring of the Year		$8.00	
The Delivery		$9.00	
Shipping and handling charge ($2.00 for first book, 50¢ for each additional)*			
Wisconsin residents must add 5.5% sales tax (on total, including shipping costs)			
TOTAL DUE			

Your name and address:

Note: If you know others who might like to have a catalog, please send us their names and addresses and we'll send them one. Thank you.

*Save on shipping! Get an order together with your friends or homeschool group. On orders of 10 or more books, shipping is only 50¢ per book. Orders of 25 or more books are shipped FREE. Just have each person write a check for their own total, send in all the checks, and indicate **one** address for shipping.